GW00383686

Minho Moments

Pam Finch

To My Keep tie
Friend Jon
Best Wishes
Pam

Acknowledgements:

Many thanks to:
Suzan Collins of Get Writing who after attending her workshop inspired me to write this collection of short stories.

Richard and Gina of the Coconut Loft Art Gallery and Coffee Lounge for their support in providing practical advice whether it be on book titles or technical problems.

Dedication:

This book is dedicated
to the memory of
Ray

CONTENTS

The Box

The box had been washed in from the night's storm. Zé noticed it as he scrambled down onto the beach. It was just what he wanted. He grabbed the rope handle and dragged it up to the wall of the quay. He saw a couple of fishermen pause from unloading their catch grinning, but ignored them. Once past the boats, he lifted the box onto his shoulder - the damp wood stained his shirt - and tried to hurry, but with his uneven walk the box knocked back and forward against his head.

Half way down the narrow lane Zé stopped, rested against the café wall and gulped in a few deep breaths; the fat dog with its short legs who had been following from the beach overtook him. At the end of the lane, Zé crossed the railway track and climbed over the sagging wire fence of his yard. He listened. Only his grandmother was at home talking back to the television.

Undecided, Zé stood in the yard. Where should he put the box? He thought the best place was under the steps of the balcony where it would be hidden by his mother's pots of geraniums.

That evening, as the family sat at the table around a cauldron of fish stew, his brother Nico said: 'Does anyone want the box that's under the steps?'

His mother paused before she handed him a bowl. Zé kept his eyes on the bowl of lumpy liquid in front of him.

'Eh?'

Paulo, another brother, the bread in his mouth muffling the words asked, 'What box? I don't know anything about a box.'

Grandmother waved her spoon at Paulo:

'Where's your manners?' she demanded.

Paulo glared at her.

'You're not too old to be told,' she continued and wiped grease from her chin.

Nico leaned back in his chair and scratched his stubble.

'This box ...'

'Eat,' their mother ordered and dropped the ladle back into the cauldron.

Later, Zé crept under the balcony and pushed the box further back behind the steps and threw a sack over it.

Zé said not a word to anyone about the box. Said nothing all the following week to the men he worked with on the road repairs. Said nothing to any of his brothers. Nothing to his mother, or his grandmother.

The day came at last. Everyone was up early and in a good mood. His sister smiled when he said she looked nice in her costume. She tossed her head and her gold earrings swung. His brothers even talked to him during breakfast, lightly teasing him, calling him '*O pequeno,*' Little one.

Later, while everyone was busy, Zé slipped out of the house and walked to the quay. All the boats had been moored close to the quay wall; green and red bunting fluttered from the masts. Nobody went fishing on *Festa* Day. Zé sat on the sea wall and threw pebbles into the water trying to make each 'plop' louder than the one before. He watched the car ferry dip and rise as it crossed the mouth of the river to Galicia. When the sun began to burn his arms he left the quay and walked home through the deserted streets.

The house was empty - everyone had left for the *Festa*. Zé changed into his best trousers and a clean shirt, then he went into his mother's bedroom and stood in front of the mirrored wardrobe door. He opened the door and unhooked his father's waistcoat. He held it at arms length and the sun, shining through the half closed shutters, caught the sheen of the red satin. Once on, the waistcoat seemed bigger than ever. Zé looked at himself in the mirror, first with the waistcoat buttoned up then undone. He tried crossing his arms; thrusting his hands in his trouser pockets; putting his thumbs in his belt. He tried the waistcoat with only the top button done up, then only the middle button, then just the bottom. Finally, he took the waistcoat off and hung it back inside the wardrobe.

Outside, he pulled the box from under the steps, swung it on to his shoulder and started up the hill to the next village. The day was hot. It was always hot for the *Festa Nossa Senhora da Boa Viagem* Festival of Our Lady for a Good Journey.

Just beyond the cross-roads he passed the house; the front wall was decorated with blue and gold tiles. Along the boundary wall a row of lemon trees overhung with blossom and both the new green and yellow ripe fruit. Two women sat on the high veranda; white crocheting jiggling in their black laps. Zé didn't notice them exchange glances and one women tap the side of her head.

At the bridge the bicycles blocked his way. Boys lounged across their handlebars smirking. Zé rested the box on the bridge wall and bent to loosen the lace of his boot. He glanced up as one of the boys walked crab-like towards him. The others whistled and rang their bells. Zé waited until they had finished their fun; then they cycled away down the hill, their arms waving in the air, and he tried not to listen to their mocking:

'*O Inválido - O Pequeno Idiota.*'

Zé lifted the box onto his shoulders and crossed the bridge. The road narrowed and turned into an uneven cobbled lane. He stepped slowly, not wanting to stumble and fall.

Twenty minutes later he walked through the arches of paper flowers and ribbons decorating the new road that led to the village church. Zé could smell the sardines grilling. Folk music throbbed from a speaker fixed to a telegraph pole. Under the speaker, girls practised dance steps; their red, green, blue skirts swinging in time to the beat. In the Square, men had set up a make-shift bar, table tops sagging with crates of beer.

Three young men arrived with a step ladder and wanted the beer stalls moved. The stalls were in the way of stringing fairy lights between an avenue of trees. An argument broke out. A knot of "catch who can catch me" children got in the way of the step ladder and the three young men forgot their argument to chase the children back to their families. Zé stopped. He lowered the box; his arm felt as though it was dead and his ear throbbed from where the wood had continuously knocked. As he watched the noisy, cheerful busyness, he felt nervous tinglings churn through his stomach which seemed to mix together with an excited squeezing in his chest. He hoped this year's *Festa* would be the *Festa* for him - it had been a long year waiting ...

A horn sounded, Zé turned and dragged his box out of the way of the doughnut van.

Zé was full: the sardines had been sweet, the doughnut sweeter and Nico, still in a good mood, came and sat on the bench near him. He put an arm around Zé's shoulder.

'My little brother, we were worried about you. Here ... don't drink it too quickly.'

Zé took the bottle and nodded a thanks as the beer scratched his throat - he thought he felt a little dizzy.

The dancing was a jumble of colours and the music louder than he could ever remember. His sister clapped her hands at him as she whirled past.

Before the dancing, there had been the procession. Village men with strong arms shouldering the floats. The statue of Our

Lady for a Good Journey stood under a glittering flowery bower lifted high for all the crowd to view. The priest walked under a purple and gold tasselled canopy; each corner fixed to a gilt pole, and carried by acolytes. Then came the service and Zé had stood a little way off from the villagers as they crowded round the church porch to listen to the priest. His mother had eventually found him, shook her head, and flicked dust from his shirt.

And his box was safe - quite safe. He had hidden it between the wall of the church and the empty beer crates. The fairy lights sparkled under a violet sky and in the Square, on a stage of trestles and boards, the local pop band performed. In their tight, torn jeans and sweat-stained tee shirts, the boys fought with their guitars. They strummed and screamed and their music vibrated across the fields. Zé stood and watched and waited and then suddenly there she was. Her scarlet skirt full and swinging with the music.

At last year's *Festa* she had smiled at him. For a full minute he had felt warm prickles run over him, then believing that the smile had been done for a joke, especially when her squealing friends had pulled her away, he turned his back. But later, as she had been leaving, she had waved to him; at least he thought the wave was for him.

Now he watched her laughing with a group of girls. She glanced over their heads, saw him and smiled a wide smile. This time he knew the smile was just for him. Zé shifted his weight. His foot throbbed. He watched her long legs hop in time to the beat; she flung out her arms and spun around and around. Her hair, worn in a plait that hung to her waist, swung like a black rope - her friends jumped out of her way. The song ended and she stopped. She put her hands on her large hips and laughed. Still Zé watched. The next tune began slow and soft. She swayed lifting her hands, her big sunburned hands, above her head and, clapping the rhythm, she chasséd towards him.

Later, when the sky was indigo and most of the fairy lights had blown their fuse, the villagers were making their own music. (The pop band had stopped playing mid-chord when the lead singer, glancing at his watch, realised the time was up on their two hour booking. The spot lights were switched off and all that was left on stage was a coil of cable.) With rolled up newspapers as bugles; knives and forks pinging on empty beer bottles, they accompanied the postman's banjo.

Zé stood in the darkness by the wall of the church. She put a hand on his shoulder. It felt warm and heavy. He looked up into her face. She smiled her wide smile.

Zé didn't think he was breathing. They stood silent. Nearby the makeshift music grew and faded as the villagers staggered around the Square.

Zé gulped, 'I'm … I'm …'

'My name's Esperança,' she said.

Esperança? His grandmother's name! *Esperança*. Hope!

'And you're Zé.'

Ze nodded. He didn't have any words. She rested her chin on the top of his head.

'You're nice,' she sighed.

Zé thought what he should say. Should he tell her how much he loved watching her dance? Should he tell her how he had been waiting so much for this year *Festa*? Should he tell her …

Zé stretched his arms round her waist and as he did so, she pulled him closer to her body. His face rested against the embroidered lace that pulled taut across her bosom. He closed his eyes. He couldn't believe this was happening.

'Zé?'

'Mmm?'

'Kiss me.'

Zé dropped his arms and stepped away.

'Oh, don't you want to?' she whispered.

Zé said nothing. He moved away and began lifting empty beer crates away from the wall; then he dragged his box to where she was still standing.

'What's that for?' she asked.

Zé didn't reply; he just stepped onto the box. Slowly their faces got closer; the tips of their noses touched. She turned a little and Zé felt her eyelash tickle his cheek.

'Oh Zé, you are clever,' she murmured.

'Me?' he snorted, 'I'm not. They call me idiot …'

'No! No! You're not. To me.. to me you are …'

'*O pequeno?*'

'Yes! Little one. My little one.'

Their lips touched. Immediately they both drew away, and then Esperança wrapped her long, strong arms around Zé for a loving kiss.

The remaining fairy lights had given into the stars. Millions of them. Before that, the fireworks had been the best yet, but even they couldn't compete with the stars.

Now over-excited children were wanting to be carried home; grumbling wives were wanting husbands to walk straight and nobody wanted to help pick up the litter.

A young couple left the *Festa de Nossa Senhora da Boa Viagem*. As they walked along the lane through the arches of paper flowers and ribbons he tried not to limp too much and she, holding his hand, balanced with ease, a box on her head.

*

None so Blind

The only time Hilary Browne had sex out of doors was on her 53rd birthday. The day had begun as any other. Donald had, as usual, set the alarm for 6.15 despite their being on holiday. After letting the clock ring for exactly twenty seconds he had switched it off, then sitting on the edge of the bed, had examined the soles of his feet before padding across into the bathroom and locking the door.

Once the bathroom door closed Hilary slid out of bed and opened the shutters. Then back between the sheets, propped up on pillows, she looked out at the jagged mauve ridge of the Serra d'Avis that lay under the early ice-white Portuguese sky. That wonderful morning view, Hilary thought some days later, should have indicated that this year's holiday would be truly memorable. (Their honeymoon, and the following twenty-eight annual holidays in August had always been spent at "The Windmill B&B" in Cromer, a seaside town perched on the bracing north Norfolk coast.)

Their breakfast table was set out on the terrace by the pool. Other guests murmured, or nodded 'Good Morning' as they sat down. Donald had made no mention of it being her birthday, but the sky was warming to forget-me-not blue and Hilary knew that this first day of their holiday was going to be full of sunshine. As Donald gulped at his orange juice, Hilary noticed a little cardboard box, brightly coloured next to the basket of rolls. Donald saw her glance, and he slid the box further behind the milk jug. Hilary relaxed back in her chair. Without her glasses she couldn't read the lettering anyway. How silly and childish of him. She reached for a banana, peeled it and began slicing it into matching pieces.

'Donald? What are we going to do today? Anything exciting?'

'Mmm?' Donald bit into his roll and tore half of it away.

'Anything special? Are we doing anything special today?'

Donald reached for the coffee pot.

'W-e-l-l,' the drawn out word made Hilary bring the knife down with a crack onto her plate and the last piece of banana shot sideways and fell on the marbled terrace. Hilary ignored it and tapped Donald's knuckles with the flat side of the knife.

'Come on. What's on the programme for

today?'

Donald pursed his lips into his own personal smile and pushed the little coloured box nearer to Hilary. She looked down at it.

'I haven't got my glasses. What is it Donald?'

'Something special. Extra special.'

He gripped the edge of the table and pushed his chair away until it was balancing on the two back legs. With his arms outstretched, he expanded his chest and Hilary saw the pale, freckly skin where his shirt buttons gaped.

'Be careful,' she said then: 'For me?'

'W-e-l-l,' Donald allowed the chair to fall forward and the jolt rocked the table. Hilary kept her eyes lowered as another couple passed by the side of them. Donald reached forward and picked up the box.

'It's taken me ages to get hold of this. The catalogues I've been through and trawling the net for hours ...'

'I know that,' interrupted Hilary.

'... but at last. It was not easy to find, you know. Not easy at all.'

He held the box under Hilary's nose. She leaned away and tried to focus the words.

'Donald. What is it?' She was aware her voice had carried over the pool, but ignored the interested glances in their direction.

'The suppliers I've been in touch with, but good ole Jameson …'

'Jameson? What has he got to do with anything?'

'Yes, good ole Jameson. Managed to get it for me just before we left home. The light will be perfect today.'

'Donald. Stop gazing at the sky. What is today?'

'Today, ole girl … ' Donald lifted the coffee pot again and shook it hopefully.

'Today is the day that Donald Browne, Vice Chairman of the East Coast Photographic Society is going to make history. Wait until they see - oh, yes - they'll be that livid. What till they see ...'

'See what?' sighed Hilary.

'Mmm? Oh, are you going? Find out if there is any more coffee will you?'

'Donald, this is not a road, it is a track ... and hire cars should not be taken onto tracks. You know that.'

Donald didn't answer. He had flattened himself over the steering wheel. They had driven through a mountain hamlet some miles back and then as the road climbed Donald had turned off - or rather, skidded off, thought Hilary. The car continued to bump over stones, twigs and last autumn's leaves, then the track began to drop.

'You're driving too fast.' Hilary arched her back from the hot seat and dragged at the neck of her blouse. She dangled her arm out of the window, but pulled it in when her hand brushed the hot door.

'And why didn't you get a car with air conditioning?'

Donald didn't reply. Hilary didn't expect him to and, as she already knew the answer, closed her eyes. With the car's jolting stop Hilary looked across at Donald. He was peering out through the windscreen and smiling. Hilary turned and looked.

'Great. Just what we need.'

The front row of sheep stared back at them. Dozens of others milled around the track; some jumped on and off the low dry- walls, others turned and set off the way they had come, before changing their minds and returning to the flock.

'Hoot your horn.'

'No. No,' said Donald. He twisted round in his seat scrabbling for his bag. By the time he stepped out onto the track, the sheep had surrounded the car. He leaned back in and pulled another bag and the tripod from the rear seat.

'Out you get,' he said draping both bags

round his neck.

Hilary closed her window, pushed at the door and peeled herself away from the car seat. Donald shuffled between the sheep and handed her the tripod.

'Wait a moment Donald. I need my hat. What about you?'

Hilary sensed his impatience as she hunted through the car door pocket.

'No. No. I'll be all right. Are you ready now?'

'Yes,' Hilary pulled at the cotton brim and hooked the tripod strap over her shoulder. 'Your bald patch will burn.'

Donald pushed through the flock, walked along the track then looked over the wall.

'Come over here.'

Hilary clung to his arm and shook grit from her sandals.

'Donald; you didn't lock the car.'

'Never mind, ole girl.'

Never mind! thought Hilary. Never mind! Never in all their years had Donald not locked the car door. What's wrong with the man today? She glanced over the wall: the ground, covered with shrubs, boulders, eucalyptus saplings, dropped steeply away. Donald sat and swung his legs over the wall. 'Now do as I ask and pass me the tripod when I'm ready.' Hilary turned; a semicircle of sheep caged her against the wall. 'Donald! They've followed us.'

'Good. Good. Everything's fine. That's what I want.'

Hilary watched Donald first edge, then slither down across the uneven ground. He wedged his feet between some tufts of grass, gained his balance and took his camera from one of the bags slung round his neck. 'Right, c'mon.'

'Donald,' Hilary knew her sigh was a waste of breath.

'Please explain.'

'This is going to be a magnificent shot. Me down here - at a very acute angle - the sheep peering over the wall. It'll be wonderful, but you're going to have to move out of the way.'

Hilary shuffled sideways.

'No! No! First pass me the tripod.'

Hilary pulled the strap over her head and began stretching the tripod towards Donald. Afterwards she tried to picture exactly what happened. She knew she had leaned over the wall as far as she could, and Donald was reaching out to catch the strap. Of course, Donald was adamant that she had let go before he had got a good grip. Whatever it was, the tripod fell, hit Donald's shin, he stumbled away and the tripod went down the mountain side, knocking and skewering between the boulders; pausing when caught in a shrub, only to tumble on down until it was out of sight. Hilary decided not to catch Donald's eye, but to wait.

'Well, come along. I'll need help to find it.'

'I can't, Donald. I just can't.'

'Yes you can.'

Donald turned; holding his camera, began slipping sideways, his knees bent for balance.

'What are you doing? Come on.'

Hilary wiped her palms down the side of her skirt, sat and swung her legs over the wall. She crouched down on the soil and clung to a bunch of young shoots. Hilary watched Donald's strides first widened and then speed up; he began slithering on, then he fell backwards onto the bracken. He carried on sliding until a boulder stopped him. He twisted round and leaned against the stone. Hilary bunched her skirt round her legs and slowly bumped herself towards him.

'Are you all right? Donald?'

He was looking at the camera. 'No damage.' He fumbled with the straps of the bag.

'Here, let me help.'

'I can manage.'

'There's no need to snap, Donald.'

Hilary wriggled up, and balanced against the boulder.

'I can't see it.'

'Well, it's down there somewhere.' Donald stood up. 'Come on.'

'Donald, do we have to? It could be anywhere.'

Hilary followed on close behind Donald; he kicked against bushes, scraped his shoes at dead foliage then he stopped. The ground was levelling out into a small pine wood.

'We'd better go different ways.'

'What!?'

'We will cover more ground. You go to the right. And look properly.'

'Donald. It's all gloomy.'

Hilary tipped back her head, 'I can't even see the sky.'

'Well, it's still there,' he said and walked on.

Hilary stepped between the tree trunks, then looked back. Donald was pushing at a log. She walked further, keeping her eyes down for the black canvas bag then stopped. It could not have fallen this far. It's ridiculous. She turned again. Where was he? Nowhere in sight. She called out; waited, called again. She shouted. Silence. What to do? Try and find him? Go on looking? Go

back? She did know the rules: when lost, stay where you are and wait to be found. She stood in the soft stillness, the dusty pine needles tickled her toes. She called again:
'Donald?'
There was no reply. She dawdled on a little further picking up pine cones then tossing them away. Suddenly, she was out from the trees; the sun warm on her arms. There was a small boulder against a large one and Hilary clambered from one to the other thinking that being higher up she might get a glimpse of Donald. No. He was nowhere to be seen. But standing on the rock she did see below her the stream; running gleaming and glossy. Water ran over and between chunks of marble; shimmering their pale pink; bunches of tiny white-starred flowers jostled across smooth pebbles lying under its surface. Hilary shouted as loud as she could: 'Donald, where … ?' then stopped. No, she wasn't going to bellow out like that - this spot was too beautiful. She sat down on the boulder; its surface hot and rough; after a moment or two she pulled off her sandals and edged herself down into the stream. The water was ice cold. Threads of emerald weed caught about her ankles; she wriggled her toes; reached down, scooped a handful of

water and threw it against her cheeks then rubbed her wet fingers round her neck. She moved her feet and they sunk into a patch of fine shingle. Then she turned and stared back up at the boulder. Like a knot twisting, her chest tightened; tingling pins and needles ran along her arms. Oh God, how was she going to climb back up? Think … Think, she told herself. No need to panic. Think ... Carrying her sandals, she paddled further along the stream to pass round the boulder looking for a spot to climb back out. A frog plopped in front of her, dived through the clear water and she watched his legs fold and stretch as he swam away. After a few minutes Hilary decided she had made the wrong decision: there seemed to be no break in the high rocks to get through onto land: she turned and waded back past the boulder. She continued splashing along to what seemed to her for ages. She thought: I'm really feeling panicky. I know I'll get out of here. I know I will. But I don't like it. Then the rocks became lower until they sloped to form a small kind of jetty. Then at last. There he was. 'Don... ' she was about to call, but it wasn't him; Donald hadn't been wearing a hat, or shorts. The man was sitting on the flat stone; his legs dangling in the water. He looked up,

'*Ola.*'

'Eh, hello.' As she got closer the man reached out and took her sandals.

'Th-thanks. Thank you.'

The man held out his hand again, Hilary grasped it and climbed up onto the rock; she stepped around leaving wet foot prints on the grey slab. The man stood, then jumped onto grass at the side of the rock. He put out his hand, but Hilary ignored it, jumped, fell forward on to her knees. Hilary took the man's hand and stood up. 'Thank you. *Obri ...obri ...* '

The man smiled: '*Obrigada.*'

'Yes. Thank you. *Obrig-a* ... Oh, dear. Sorry.'

The man rummaged in the canvas satchel he had hanging across his chest. He pulled out a paper bag offering it to Hilary.

Cherries? Cherries! This is ridiculous! Utterly ridiculous! Why, thought Hilary, am I not scared? I ought to be, but I'm not, but ... but ... I've got to find Donald.

'I'm lost,' said Hilary, 'My husband ... is looking for a tripod ... I went the other way ... I've got to find the road ... no ... no ... I've got to find my husband ... it's not a road, it's a track ... our car …'

Hilary realised the man did not understand what she was saying. Oh God, this is awful.

Try actions. Hilary mimed taking photos. The man nodded and smiled. Hilary then mimed driving a car, making a vroom vroom noise. The man nodded again as though in agreement. Hilary did the driving action again and stretched her palm towards him. The man shook his head, pointed to the grass and Hilary saw a shepherd's crook. Feeling a fool Hilary started saying 'B-a-a.'

The man nodded and gave a thumbs up sign. So, thought Hilary, he's a shepherd - his flock must have been those on the track, but how do I get back up there? Hilary pointed first skywards, then to herself and then the man. He nodded. So what does that mean? She put her hand out for her sandals. The man sat down beside her and stretched his legs across the shallow grassy edge of the stream and flapped his feet in the water while she pulled on her sandals. He took a cherry from the bag, swilled it in the water and handed it to her. She bit into the ripe fruit, spat the stone into her palm, tossed it into the stream and watched it skim away out of sight. Now let me work this out, thought Hilary as she buckled her sandals: this shepherd must go back to the sheep soon - he's obviously having a crafty cool-down here by the stream, so when he starts moving, I'll follow. The shepherd offered her the bag of fruit. Hilary chose one; it was a double stem and, as she thought afterwards in a moment of ... not madness, but what ... silliness? ... happiness? had hooked the pair of cherries over her ear - just like she had done as a kid. The man peered into the bag found another double stem and tucked them around his ear. They looked at each other and laughed. She shook her head and the soft fruit bobbed against her cheek. 'Ear-rings,' she said, and up tipped the bag. She found and looped another pair over her other ear. 'Ear-rings,' she said again

'Ear-r-r-ings,' the man repeated. Hilary nodded, then thought he probably now thinks that's the English word for cherries.

Hilary squeezed her eyes shut, turned her face up to the sky; her hat dropped. She rubbed her damp forehead and flicked at her hair. She looked at the man - he had placed his hat and canvas bag by his crook. They shared out the cherries, counting each claret coloured fruit with one another. One. *Uma*. Two. *Dois*. Three. *Tres*. Four. *Quatro*. When the last stone had been competitively tossed into water, the man took Hilary's hand. The sunburnt fingers were not as rough as she had imagined. Above the stream first one dragonfly appeared, then another and another; their turquoise bodies turning and swooping, and then, just as suddenly, they were gone. She put his warm palm across her chin; his hand took the weight of her head. His beard tickled her lobe as he bit off one of the cherries. She moved to him and her mouth pulled the cherries from his ear. He laid his hand on her knees and gently rubbed at the grass stains; then he noticed some grazes; bent and kissed them. Hilary touched his head; the curls were the shade of copper. When he looked at her she saw that his eyes were speckly green; and his eyebrows were definitely golden. And the sky was … ? Hilary was undecided as to what blue it actually was when she thought about it afterwards, but knew she would always see the colour in her mind as she laid in the grass, the man's lips touching her neck. She helped him undo her blouse. His kisses moved over her breasts and his fingers tickled across her ribs. She tugged her skirt away and his palms slid along her thighs. His weight was comforting and the flesh of his chest and hips warm against her skin.

Later, Hilary thought she heard the bleating first, but perhaps he had, and ignored it. It grew louder and they both sat up. He held her close to him then took the other pair of cherries from her ear. He bit into one and put the other close to her mouth for her to eat, then collecting his crook, hat and bag, moved away and waited for her. He led her towards the pine wood, and once there onto a cobbled path. They walked in single file until the path forked when he stopped, touched his chest and pointed to the right, then lifting her hand first to his lips held it up towards the other path. Hilary gripped his elbow; and saw his muscles tighten. She stared at him, then released his arm, turned and started along the path. It began to rise first slowly, then more steeply. Hilary climbed on; when she stopped to catch her breath, she looked up and saw the wall. She scrambled on, her skirt snagging brambles until she reached the top and rolled herself over the wall. On the track she looked one way, then the other. The car! There was the car. She yanked at the door and fell into the seat. She pulled down the sun visor and looked at her face in the mirror. She didn't look any different. She put her head back and closed her eyes.

'So you didn't you find it?' Donald's voice was too loud.

Hilary fastened her seat belt. Donald threw his bags onto the back seat.

'It was all your fault.'

'Sorry.'

'Now I'll have to buy another one. More expense. It was damned stupid of you.'

'Was it?' Hilary lent back and closed her eyes again.

Donald fumbled with the ignition key.

'C'mon. No sleeping, ole girl. Need help to get off this track. I see the sheep have gone. I wonder where to.'

'Yes,' said Hilary. 'I wonder where.'

'Donald, I can't help it. They'll put the gate number up when they're ready.'

She opened her bag and checked the boarding cards for a second time. Donald took a newspaper and a folder from his rucksack.

'Want to look at it?' he asked handing her the newspaper.

Hilary turned the paper to the crossword. Donald's chuckle stopped her as she hunted for a pen. He had the folder open on his lap and was shuffling through the photographs.

'Look at these. Just look. Wonderful way I caught the light. This was an unusual church; and this one as well.'

Donald placed one photo after another on top of the crossword.

'Now this church … '

'Donald … '

'I was right you know.'

'Right?'

'Finding that place to print these photos. I'll be able to take them round to Jameson tomorrow ...'

'Donald, we wasted a whole day tramping around that hot town looking for the printers.'

'We found it in the end though, didn't we ole girl, so not wasted at all. Look at the shade I captured on this church and ... '

'Donald!'

'Ha! Jameson. Jameson. What will you say?'

Hilary went to hand the photos back when one slipped from her lap.

'Careful.'

'Sorry. sorry.' As Hilary picked the photo up Donald glanced at it.

'No, that's not of interest. Some chap I saw when we were out hunting for the tripod.'

'Oh?'

'Do you remember? You got lost or went the wrong way didn't you?'

'Did I?'

Donald was packing the photos away in the folder.

'Think he was a shepherd or something.'

He looked up at the Departure Board. 'Ah,

yes. Gate 23. Open. C'mon.'

Hilary stood, swung her bag over her shoulder and tucked the photo in the side pocket.

Donald turned and pulled at Hilary's arm.

'Hurry up ole girl. Must get in the queue. Holiday's over you know.'

'Yes Donald it is.'

*

The Way Fire Destroys

As soon as he opened the shutters he heard Miguel whistling. Sharp, bright notes from a TV advert. He pulled on his trousers, shirt and padded downstairs to the kitchen. At the sink he held his head under the cold tap. His mother was pouring milky coffee into a bowl. He sat at the table and held out his hand for the chunk of bread.

'Will you finish the field today?' Ignoring the question, he dunked his bread into the coffee.

'If it isn't finished you …'

'What?'

His mother turned away, picked up a bucket and went out to the yard. She left the door open and the early morning glare gashed his eyes. He scraped back his chair and kicked the door shut. The door hit the jamb and swung open again. In the doorway he watched his mother by the rabbit boxes chattering and cooing them as though they were her grandchildren. He stepped into his boots; as he tied them, a lace broke. His mother came, stooped down, pulled and threaded and fussed over the boots.

'There you are - that's all right now.' She looked up,' The field ... I mean ... you will try.'

He walked across the yard and dragged open the metal gates. His mother ran to help; she wedged them with stones. In the shed, the bullock sensed his bad temper; and aggravated it by being more contrary than usual whilst being harnessed into the shafts. He then led the bullock and cart across the yard; at the gate he ignored his mother as she handed him the mattock. Once outside he waited as she pushed the gates shut.

'*Adeus*,' she called.

He started along the lane; the cart wheels creaked. His boots and the bullock's hooves kicked up puffs of dry earth. He broke a switch from the hedgerow and, with each plodding step, gave the animal a vicious swipe.

The sky was changing from its early brittle white to blue. It was getting hot and he had forgotten his hat. Why hadn't his mother remembered his hat? He rubbed a fist across his throbbing eyes. He had drunk too much in the bar last night but it had been a good match. Porto had won 3-2. You needed to celebrate after watching such a game. A tune came into this head. He kicked at a stone; the suddenness made the bullock stop. It was the tune that Miguel had been whistling; that same tune from that TV advert. The bullock reared as the switch landed again and again across his flank. Miguel! Miguel! Miguel! Then his path was blocked. Sheep pushed and jostled him, but as quickly as they appeared, with the sound of the shepherd's call, the sheep frisked, turned and tumbled away down into the valley.

When he reached the fork in the lane he stopped. He felt weary. He sat on the granite plinth of the crucifix. Last night in the bar, there had been gossip, nods and winks, but he had ignored it . How his head hurt; and his throat; and his eyes.

Once, he and Miguel had been like brothers; practically twin brothers, for there had only been three days between their births. Both the only son in a family of daughters so, better than brothers, conspirators in a world of women. Their fathers had both worked year after year in Brazil; returning home only in August like all emigrants. The boys became used to being first special, then spoiled. With their silky black curls and long dark lashes they were the darlings of both families. They ran in and out of each other's homes; they shared each other's food. Either mother's laps were a comfort when they grazed a knee or bumped a head. At school, all the sisters were ready to re-write their exercises; make excuses for bad behaviour; cover up truancy. Everyone in the village saw the two of them as one. It was no good just wanting one boy to carry a basket of grapes, or help shake down the olives - you had to have the two or neither.

The first change came in their lives when he was eleven. That August his father didn't return from Brazil. Aunts and sisters huddled and whispered during the long, hot days. His mother, always in black, seemed to become buried under more crepe, but there was no talk of a funeral, no memorial services at the church; the priest never called. That autumn he was made to help with the harvesting. Playing with Miguel had to wait. The following spring it was planting. In the field one day as he stood to stretch his back, Miguel sailed past on a shining new bicycle. During the next few years he and Miguel sometimes kicked a football on the way home from school; or spent the occasional Sunday afternoon trapping and hunting in the woods, but then it was Miguel who didn't have time to meet. He was studying; he was going to go to college. He learned of Miguel's college success the day the last of his sisters married. All his sisters had married men from the town and had left the village. Now there was just him and his mother. It was on his 25th birthday when he saw the daffodil yellow Mercedes roar across the village square. He knew Miguel's father had returned from Brazil for good. Miguel was in the passenger seat; he waved. The next time he saw the car, Miguel was driving. Miguel came back from the city when his father died. All the villagers agreed he was a country boy at heart. You could tell that by the success he had made of all the land his father had acquired. And he brought a wife home. A real stunner, but a worker. What a success story. What a success!

Yesterday, sitting on the porch, his mother plucked at her Sunday black apron.
  'Son, it is the only way.'
  'No. No. I won't have it.'
  'But it's a good offer.'
  'NO!'
  'Yes,' replied his mother. 'I've said yes.'
  'You had no right! The land is mine. Mine!'
  'No, son.'
  'What do you mean No, son?'

He kicked at the porch step. A dozing cat woke and ran into the house.

'No, I mean, it was mortgaged.'

'What?'

'How else would your sisters have married?'

He stepped into the dimness of the kitchen, poured a glass of brandy, drank then belched.

His mother continued: 'But we can keep one field and ...'

'One? One?'

'... and he'll buy all our crops direct. We have nothing ... nothing to worry ...'

'You are right!' he shouted, 'We HAVE nothing.'

'Son, listen. Miguel ...'

'DON'T speak of him.' His voice loud and cracked stopped the old woman.

When he woke he knew it was late. Really it was time to go back home for some lunch, and he hadn't even reached his field. He knew his mother was right. If he wanted to get a good price, the cabbages had to be harvested today. Miguel had insisted. He caught the bullock's reins and tugged the animal away from the verge. He had to get to his field - his cabbages. He must harvest his cabbages today. The sun was stinging his neck and arms as they climbed the narrow path - he put a hand to his pounding head, but his curls were too hot to touch.

Then he saw it. Barring his way. Sparkling in the sun; the paintwork bluer than the sky. Big, black domineering wheels; their smug treads new and unworn. The little cushioned seat - pert and inviting. The engine purring like a contented cat. He stared at the tractor, then turned and looked down the steep slope to the fields. Everywhere was green: the terraced vines; the pine trees; his cabbages. The green shimmered. He closed his eyes as scalding bubbles squeezed from his lids. He rubbed his knuckles across his wet cheeks and looked again at the tractor. Its newness mocked him. Envy began to singe his body - it scorched his stomach and heart. It burnt his muscles, sinews, bones. Hot pumping blood hammered his brain. His mind blistered in the heat. Envy kindled a fire in his spirit so fierce that the blaze took hold and destroyed his soul.

He stood by the tractor and looked at its polished steering wheel. Then the dials with its cocky bright numbers. He saw Miguel slowly walking up the path. He grasped the brake - the hot metal stung his palm. His grip tightened; there was sweat between his fingers. He jumped back as the tractor began to roll. He looked down the path. Miguel, his head bent, was climbing towards the field. The tractor's engine whined, then growled. The tractor began bumping down the path gaining speed; its huge wheels turning faster and faster. It roared forward, knocked against the trunk of a cork tree, shuddered for a moment, then carried on. It hit the post leading to his field of cabbages; swerved in the mud grooves of the baked earth, rocked, turned onto his bit of land and tipped over. He smelt petrol. He saw the smoke rise, first thin and grey then becoming a black moving shape. Suddenly flames, gold and purple spurted out from the smoke; they slithered away from the burning tractor, sped across the field; racing away in every direction. He watched his crop of cabbages become a charred mess. He stood until there was silence, then he thought he heard Miguel ... whistling.

Hadith: "Beware of jealousy for verily it destroys good deeds the way fire destroys wood." Abu Dawud

*

As Sages Say

The king was thrown onto the table. Carlos groaned, pushed back his chair and tossed his cards onto the pile.

'I'm out,' he said.

Cigarette smoke mingled with the warm steamy air in the Bar Rosinha that Saturday afternoon. The storm had died; the rain had eased off, but the card players roared with glee or bawled angry shouts across the tables, as if the water was still hammering on the roof. Later, the young men hunted under the tables for crash helmets and jackets; jeered and cheered the winners and losers; slapped Carlos on the shoulder and left. Carlos tidied and stacked away the playing cards and took them over to the counter. At the door he wiped a dry circle on the glass. Just about stopped, he decided and took his umbrella from the plastic tub.

'Carlos?'

He turned and saw the bar owner standing by the pin-ball machine.

'*Sim*?'

The owner shrugged and straightened the chairs around the tables. Carlos paused, then stepped outside.

The grey sky was low over the village. A sharp wind whipped up bundles of the still spitting rain and flung them at Carlos. He shivered and opened his umbrella. Jumping around the pot holes of water from the week's rain, he trudged the narrow road-way up from the bar. The higher he climbed, the stronger the wind. He pushed the shaft of the umbrella into his neck; the ribs were straining to turn the umbrella inside out. Carlos kept to the middle of the road; down from the mountains, overflowing streams were running in fast rivulets towards him. With his head buried under the umbrella he wasn't sure it was a car hooting, but then he turned. The car was long and low and ruby red. He stepped to the side and water lapped round his ankles. As the car hummed past, fingers pale and slender, with nails the same bright red, flashed for a moment by the side window. Carlos watched the red bodywork move with ease up the hill and disappear into the mist.

'Wow,' thought Carlos.

His trainers squelched as he followed the car. At the junction, by the village refuse bins, he turned onto the cobbles between the terraces. Here the high stretched vines sheltered him from the wind, but the rain became heavy and solid again. His jeans stuck cold to his legs. He edged along the wall of the *Quinta de Flores;* saturated shell-pink hydrangeas, growing from the brickwork, threw handfuls of raindrops onto his umbrella until he reached the overhang of its large porch. He sheltered for a moment leaning against the metal gates and thought about the woman and the car. He ticked off all the families; there wasn't anyone new in the village. Once past the boundary of the *Quinta*, he took the left hand fork; immediately the path began to dip - the incline was steep and Carlos' feet slithered over the wet stones. His strides quickened until he was jogging fast. He pulled the umbrella down onto his head and, watching out for loose cobbles, he felt himself skim down the water-logged path. He was all but running when he reached the bridge.

Instinct made him reach out and grab a branch, but all he grasped were long waving tendrils of vines; they broke and he flung them away. He swerved to the side of the path and the wet grass slowed his speed; he stumbled, hit and bounced alongside a wall. There was a gap where stones had crumbled away and he stretched out his arms and fell forward between the gap. Through the rain he watched his umbrella bowl along, fall into the river, float past the mill, then disappear over the waterfall. Carlos clung to wall and waited for his gasping breath to slow down. He pushed himself around leaned against the wall and looked where the bridge should have been. It was still there he was sure; the ancient flat granite had withstood worse storms. The stone slabs were under the muddy, foaming river that roared down from the mountains. One side of the bridge was the parapet, on the other, the waterfall. Branches and shrubs swirled past and were caught on the parapet. Carlos watched to judge how much of it was submerged, Should he risk it? He had known deeper flooding but the force and speed of the rushing logs and up-rooted plants showed that one slip and he'd go the same way as his umbrella.

The rain became lighter. Suddenly it switched off. Carlos looked up towards the ridges and already streaks of blue were pushing through the grey. Quickly the blue spread out and Carlos felt the sun's warmth on his wet tee-shirt. He looked at his cut hands and grazes on the inside of his arms. He shook one, then the other, sodden foot.

If he hadn't been such a mild-mannered boy, he most probably would have sworn, but ... the cuts would heal; the sun was drying him and there were more umbrellas at home. He needed to think, but Carlos wasn't a greater thinker, but he thought of the long climb back up to the bar and the cadging of a lift home round by the village outskirts. He then thought again about the red car, and the red finger nails.

The last of the grey sky had disappeared and the late afternoon sun glistened the green vines and shone the cobbles. The noise of the river drowned the squeaking and it was only when, with reluctance Carlos pushed himself from the wall to start the climb back to the café he saw, a few paces in front of him, the pair of bullocks. They halted and the squeaking stopped. The animals swung away from each other, lowered their heads and munched the damp grass at the base of the wall. Carlos' way was barred; the high wooden yoke blocked his view.

He called: '*Ola*?'

No reply.

'*Ola*?' This time louder. He waited, then stooped and peering through the legs of the bullocks, saw a pair of rubber boots.

'*Oooolaaa*?' he shouted.

The bullocks, in unison, looked up and fixed him a stare. Carlos took his chance and pushed between a flank and the wall. The girl was scraping the floor of the cart with a long handled shovel.

'The river ... it's high ...' began Carlos.

'I know. What do you expect? There's been a storm.'

The girl dropped the shovel down into the cart, took a stick and flicked it towards the animals. They moved forward and the squeaking began again. Carlos sniffed.

The bullocks stopped by the river. The girl said impatiently:

'Get up then.'

Carlos put his back against the tail of the cart, pushed on his hands and lifted himself onto the cart.

'Manure,' he grumbled.

'So?'

The girl wrapped the reins across her shoulders and secured them under her arms. She climbed onto the first narrow piece of the parapet and watched the water break around her boots. She waited. Slowly, she edged along, pushing against the swirling river.

The bullocks paced by her side over the submerged bridge. One bellowed a complaint and the girl reached down, held onto the yoke and murmured to the animal. Carlos drew up his knees and held his nose.

The cart stopped and Carlos looked around. A pine log was caught on the parapet. He watched as the girl first tugged it from the water, then kick it into the river. He watched as she pulled her skirts tightly round her thighs, then duck and climb under the branches of the pines, jerking the reins to encourage the bullocks to keep moving. They were halfway across the river, the water was deeper, the roar louder. One of the animals hesitated. Carlos thought of the large gaps between the slabs. The cart wheels turned slowly, then there was a jolt and the bullocks stopped. Carlos saw the girl peer down through the muddy torrent and shake her head. Carlos wondered what he should do. The girl patted, whispered to the animal, tugged the yoke once, twice, whispered again and pulled at the reins. The animals strained for a moment, rested, then slowly the cart began to move, and continued on through the water to the lane on the other side. Carlos jumped off the cart. The girl unwound the reins and the bullocks continued plodding on.

'I don't know you,' he said to the girl.

'No. You don't,' she replied.

Carlos thought she was not being very helpful.

'Look,' mumbled Carlos, 'I mean thanks ... I mean I would like to see you again.'

'You will.'

'I will?'

'Bar Rosinha It's my Grandad's.'

'Your Grandad's?' Carlos couldn't think of anything else to say.

'Y-e-s. I'm up from Porto. To help Granny for a while.'

'I didn't know there was anyone new in the village.'

'Well, there is. Me.'

'Oh.'

'It's the fields and everything. Getting too much for Granny.'

The bullocks stopped by a gate. The girl ran and opened it, and the animals turned into the field. The girl followed, dragging the shovel off the cart. Carlos came and stood by the gate. For the first time the girl smiled. Carlos looked at her bright brown eyes and her wide mouth.

'I really would like to see you again,' said Carlos.

'Okay,' said the girl and a shovelful of manure landed by his feet.

Though there were still pot holes in the road and up-rooted trees along the river bank by the next Saturday the storm had been forgotten. The sun was shining as Carlos walked through the village. Opposite the bar was a garage, and parked on the forecourt a car: long and low and glinting red in the sunlight. As Carlos passed, the car door opened and a tall, slim woman climbed out. Carlos never noticed her as he hurried into the Bar Rosinha.

As sages say, oft a little morning rain foretells a pleasant day - Charlotte Brontë.

*

Teatime with Cinza

The ambulance shot along the lane, missed the gates, backed up then pulled in and stopped on the cobbled patio. A policeman came out of the house and indicated to the driver to reverse down through a gap in the trees to the caravan. Two more police appeared and followed the ambulance; one talking on a mobile phone, the other pushing aside twigs and leaves with a stick. The caravan door opened, a policeman climbed out and fastened back the door.

'All yours,' he said as the medics left their cab and went into the caravan.

The police stood silent until the one had finished the phone call; he then said:

'It's going to be a difficult one. Going to involve a lot of people ... a lot of departments.'

'And a lot of paperwork,' interrupted the policeman who started swishing his stick amongst the fallen leaves again.

'How many are in the house with him?' asked the officer who had come out of the caravan.

'Two. Silva and a local man, off-duty; he lives in the village. He was here just by chance. Made the call.'

One of the medics jumped down from the caravan steps and opened the rear doors of the ambulance. He looked across at the police and first held his hand up and then turned it down.

'As I thought,' said the policeman, 'Knew one had had it; wasn't sure about the other. Couldn't see anything for the blood. I'd better be at the house. You two okay here?'

He acknowledged their nods.

'Forensics are on their way,' he called and walked back through the small plantation of beech and oak. He crossed the patio and went into the house; ducked his head and stepped into a large kitchen. The evening sun had moved from the one window and now, dropped behind the mountains, the room was dark and dismal. By the door the policeman switched on the light. From the ceiling a pale orange glow fell onto the table. Silva was standing by the cooker; the off-duty officer sat at the table, opposite the man, writing. He stood up and handed the policeman a sheet of paper.

'Will this do for now? I'm on duty later and will formalise everything with my superior.'

The policeman took the paper, folded in half. As the off-duty officer walked to the door, he whispered to Silva.

'Someone needs to sort out what's in the stable.'

A flash of yellow crossed the window as a second ambulance passed the house. The off-duty officer closed the door behind him. Silva pushed himself away from the cooker and stood in the middle of the kitchen. The policeman unfolded the sheet of paper; scanned the writing and after a few minutes said to the man:

'Look at me.'

In the silence Silva's boots scraped the stone floor.

The man lifted his head for a moment, then he crossed and laid his arms on the table and dropped his forehead onto them.

'*Senhor - Senhor.*'

The policeman swung a chair out from the table, sat down and brushed pastry crumbs onto the floor.

'I want you to tell me what has happened here today.'

***

Gordon's Renault coughed to a stop; several lengths of wood slid from the roof down in front of the windscreen, hit the bonnet, then fell to the ground. Gordon slammed the car door and untied the rest of the wood letting them drop around his feet.

'Do you need as much as that?' Alex, hearing the car had walked up from his caravan.

'Got them cheap.'

Alex kicked the wood together. 'Will you get it finished today?'

'I will if you could make the effort to help. It's for your benefit.'

'Yes I know Dad. Thanks, but I've got to take Cinza for a good ride. We've got get to know each other ...'

'Please yourself - only don't call me "Dad". I was your Mother's husband. Nothing more.'

'Okay. Okay ... Gordon. Thought I'd go up as far as the peak.'

'Just give me a hand to get this wood under the vines and then bugger off.'

Later that morning when Alex rode Cinza in from the lane, he heard Gordon shouting.

'*Sim. Sim.* I can let you have two cases for fifty Euros, or three for sixty.'

Alex let the horse loose; it trotted across the grass; Alex walked round to the back of the house. Gordon switched off his mobile and grinned.

'Another done deal.'

'Another local ripped off?'

'Yep.'

Gordon picked up the lump hammer and swung it down onto a stake.

Alex said: 'When I was out riding I saw a huge fire in the valley.'

Gordon shrugged.

'Right, that's the last one. And now you're here, you can help lift the panels into place. Won't take long.'

'What do you think the fire was?'

'Some immigrant come back home trying to clear land to build on, I expect.'

'Oh, I see. Anyway, thanks for doing this ... Gordon.'

The older man grunted.

'I do appreciate it and Cinza does need a kinda shelter.'

Gordon stared at Alex, then walked away. His mobile rang and Alex heard him shouting: 'Ten Euros' and 'Two for the price of one'.

Alex stacked together odd lengths of wood and collected up the nails. He was hunting for a broom when he heard Portuguese shouting and the horse neighing; he ran round to the front of the house.

'Catrina! Catrina! What's happening?'

The girl pointed to a narrow strip of earth by the side of the grass. Amongst the hoof prints were broken stems and flattened leaves.

'*Meus girassois - meus girassois* - now they'll never grow.'

'Yes, they will, they will.'

Alex led the horse away and looped the reins over the fence.

He knelt on the grass, tidied the bristly leaves and smoothed over the earth.

'There,' he smiled up at the girl, 'As good as new.'

'*O quê?*'

'Your sunflowers; they will grow and grow and grow.' Alex stood and held his hand above his head, 'Taller, than me.'

Catrina smiled.

'What's going on?'

Gordon ambled round from the side of the house. He pulled from his back pocket a packet of tobacco and looked from Alex to the girl.

'D'yer hear me? What's going on?' He rolled some tobacco into the paper, 'Well?'

'Nothing,' said Alex, 'Nothing. Catrina was a bit upset - about her sunflowers.'

'Flowers!' Gordon slid the paper across his lips. He went up to the girl and squeezed her buttocks. 'Indoors - *casa.*' He nodded his head towards the kitchen door.

'Now wait a minute Da ... Gordon. What do you think you're doing? Catrina is ...'

'Catrina, is it? Only been here a couple of days and we've got very friendly.'

'Yes. I have and I don't like what I see.'

'Oh, so he doesn't like what he sees,' Gordon pulled a thread of tobacco from his tongue, 'And what might that be?'

Alex turned towards Catrina, but she had gone into the house.

He said: 'I think you've over stepped the mark.'

Gordon looked at Alex, but didn't reply. He shook his lighter trying to get a flame. When he had lit the roll-up he inhaled; smoke blew into Alex's face and said:

'Catrina is here to housekeep. Nothing more.'

He inhaled again, trying to keep the cigarette alight.

'It makes me wonder how you treated Mum.'

'Don't bring your mother into this. I looked after your mother well right up to the end.'

'All right. All right. Sorry.'

'Anyway don't worry about her. She's not your concern. It's the language ... a little English ...   a little Portuguese.'

60

'Your Portuguese should be good. You've lived here long enough.'

Gordon flicked his lighter again.

'You just concentrate on your holiday.'

He pulled his phone from his shirt pocket.

'You're done with university and studying and everything else, so just have a good time with your horse until it's time for you to bugger off back to the UK and get a job.'

'I've told you ... I've got a job ... a good position ... I'm just waiting ...'

Gordon walked away punching the keys on the phone.

Alex stood in the garden and ate the sandwich that Catrina had made for him, then he wandered into the makeshift stable and sat on an upturned bucket next to Cinza. He leaned his cheek against the horse; its warm flesh made him want to close his eyes and drift away. The horse moved and Alex looked up.

'Hi Catrina. Are you and Cinza friends now?'

'*Desculpe*?'

'Only a joke Catrina. Here, give him a pat.'

The girl stood still and looked from Alex to the horse.

Alex held the girl's arm and smoothed her hand over the horse's neck. The horse tossed his head; Catrina pulled away and stepped back.

'It's all right,' laughed Alex, and ruffled its mane. Catrina reached out and touched the horse's soft, grey hair. Alex looked at Catrina's wrist; thin and sunburnt. A chain with silver charms swung as she moved her hand across the horse.

'That's nice,' he said.

Catrina picked at one of the charms.

'A horse shoe.' Alex pointed down to Cinza's hoofs.

'*Sim*. Yes. *A sapata do cavalo.*'

Alex fumbled over the Portuguese words; Catrina said them again slowly. She turned the chain round her wrist and held another charm between her finger and thumb.

Alex said: 'A boot,' and lifted his foot.

Catrina laughed: 'A boot,' and as she lifted her leg, her sandal slipped off. Alex knelt in the straw, and holding Catrina's ankle she wriggled her toes back into the sandal.

'Look at Prince Charming,' Gordon stood in the doorway, his bulky shape spoiling the sunlight.

Alex stood up. 'Catrina's just getting to know Cinza.'

'Well, isn't that nice.'

'Do you have to be so ...'

Gordon stepped past Alex and put his face close to the girl's: words spat from his mouth. Alex thumped Gordon's shoulder.

'What are you saying? Leave her alone.'

Gordon turned and caught Alex in the chest with his elbow; the boy lost his balance, fell and knocked the upturned bucket. It rolled out through the doorway and rocked to a stop on the cobbles. As Catrina ran past Gordon, he lifted his fist to her, then laughed and patted the horse's flank.

'Get up for Christ's sake,' he pushed his foot against Alex's thigh. 'Find something useful to do.'

From his caravan Alex walked up to the house, The Renault wasn't in the yard. As he passed the kitchen window he saw Catrina at the sink. He knocked on the glass and she lifted the sash.

'Gordon?' he asked.

She raised her shoulders 'Ville São Jorge?'

Alex went to the stables and led Cinza out. The horse danced on the grass.

'No. No. We're not going anywhere yet, but this evening we'll go and watch the sunset.'

Alex rubbed his forehead against Cinza's nose. The horse eyed him. Alex laughed.

'Come on over by the fence and no trampling the flowers.'

Catrina stood by the back door holding up a bottle

'Oh, yes. Thank you, Catrina.'

Alex sat at the kitchen table and sipped his beer. On the table were half a dozen apples – their crimson skins brushed with yellow. Alex saw himself ten – fifteen years ago, again sitting at a kitchen table as his mother peeled apples; the skin coiling down from the flesh and him trying to catch the spiral and hoping it wouldn't break.

He fetched a knife from a drawer and began peeling one of the apples. Catrina stood watching. As he reached the last piece of the peel he bounced the coil. Catrina laughed, found a knife and they both competed in trying to produce the longest length of peel. Then Alex chopped the apples and put them in a saucepan of water.

'Apple crumble,' he said.

'*O Quê?*'

He didn't answer, but went to the cupboard and found flour and sugar. Catrina guessed and fetched butter from the frig. Between them, with floury hands, spilt sugar and boiled over apples on the hob, they made the pudding.

Steam rose as the sink filled with hot water; Alex chased a wasp out of the window with the tea towel; then they heard the car. Alex went to the back door.

'Hi. You'll be pleased – made a ...'

Gordon stood by the car.

'Why isn't that horse in the stable?'

'He likes the sunshine.'

Gordon grunted and opened the boot.

'Want a hand?'

Alex stood by the car as Gordon lifted out a cardboard box.

'Out of the way.' He pushed past and walked into the house. Alex followed.

'What the hell has been going on?'

He dropped the box onto the rocking chair; the runners rattled on the uneven slabs.

'We've made an apple crumble.'

Alex stood at the table between Gordon and Catrina.

'Stay out of the house.'

'What?'

'You heard. You've got your caravan. You can come here to eat and that's all.'

'Gordon, what's the matter for heaven's sake. You're nuts.'

Gordon lunged at Alex, twisted his arm behind his back and shoved him towards the door.

'Pack it in you idiot. What am I – under arrest?'

Catrina ran forward; Gordon swung out his arm and she put her hands to her face and crouched down by the sink.

Alex turned fast around and stepped away.

'Pack it in. Just calm down.'

Gordon picked up the box and went out into the hall.

Alex filled the kettle and lit a gas ring.

'Catrina, go into the garden.' He paused and found the word: '*Jardim*.'

She nodded and ran out of the kitchen. Alex opened the oven door; juice was bubbling over the edge of the dish and the crumble topping was toffee brown. He turned off the gas, set out three mugs and dropped a teabag in each. The kettle softly whistled; he called out.

'Gordon. Come and have a drink.'

He went to the back door. Catrina stood by the horse picking leaves from of a bush of rosemary. He put his arm round her shoulder.

'*Chá*?' he said.

The three sat at the table. Gordon rolled a cigarette, then put it behind his ear. Catrina pulled a loose thread from the hem of her tee shirt.

Alex said: 'I don't know what's going on, but you invited me here for a holiday and .... well, it's hardly a holiday atmosphere.'

Gordon jigged the tea bag up and down in his mug.

'All you've got to do is be here with your horse, and mind your own business about everything else."

'Why?'

'Cos I said so.'

'Let's eat the crumble.' Alex put the pudding on the table. Catrina fetched dishes and spoons and Gordon lit his cigarette.

'Gordon!'

He mumbled an obscenity and pinched out the cigarette. Alex scooped some of the crumble into dish and slid it across the table to Catrina.

'Thank – you,' she whispered.

Alex shared out the rest of the pudding and said: '*Bom Apetite*.'

Gordon grunted. 'Just let's eat the stuff shall we?'

In the silence, spoons scraped at the dishes; then a fanfare of military music and Gordon pulled the phone from his pocket and went into the hall.

Suddenly metal clanked on the stone slabs; a clattering echoed through the house and Alex stacking the dishes in the sink turned and laughed.

'Oh, Cinza. Cinza. What are you doing here?'

The horse side-stepped across the kitchen. Catrina put her hands to her mouth and giggled.

The horse tossed his head; kicked out and his back legs hit the dresser door. Alex hung his arms round the horses neck.

'Come on, outside. There's no apple crumble left for you.'

'Christ Almighty!'

Gordon came from the hall, swinging a walking stick; he threshed it above his head then brought it down on the horse's back. The horse reared and his neigh was like a baby's cry. Alex grabbed the stick, and tried pulling it from Gordon's hands, but he wouldn't let go and Alex dragged him across the room. Gordon stumbled against a chair and fell; the horse reared again; his hooves hitting the table top. Gordon stood up spun and lifted the chair; he cracked it against the horse's face.

'Catrina screamed '*Nao. Nao.*' the words lost in gulping sobs.

Gordon then swung the chair towards her, but she ran behind the table and into the hall. Alex, head down, charged into him, punching at his chest. Gordon grabbed Alex's shirt and tried to fling him away, but Alex hooked a foot behind his leg and gave him a shove. On the floor he rolled onto his side and tried to stand up; Alex pushed him down.

'Catrina. Go down to the caravan and stay there.'

There was no reply. Alex shouted again:

'Caravan.'

He heard the front door open and click shut.

Alex stoked his hands across the horse's neck, face, back. He tried to encourage it to turn towards the kitchen door, but his hoofs stamped the stone floor. Alex looked at Gordon sitting in the rocking chair.

'What the hell's up with you?'

Gordon took a cigarette from his pocket, lit it and coughed.

'Did Mum have to put up with this?'

'Get that animal out of the house.'

'I will. But I asked you a question about Mum.'

Gordon pushed back in the chair, lifted his feet and the chair swung forward.

'Listen you little shit. This is my house and I say what happens. Get it out.'

'Yes. But Cinza's frightened.'

'Do it.'

'All right. All right.'

Alex whispered and petted and slowly led the horse out to garden and to the stable. When he returned, Gordon was sitting at the table holding an empty glass, he poured another whisky lifted it to his mouth and said:

'Now go and fetch the whore.'

'What?'

'You heard. Go and get her. I want something to eat. Something proper.'

'No. I won't.'

Gordon swallowed the whisky and refilled the glass.

'This is what's going to happen. You are going to get her. She is going to do as she is told.'

His walking stick was on the table; he stretched out his hand and his fingers tapped along the handle.

'You are then going to stay in the caravan and tomorrow I'm getting rid of the horse and you can clear off back to the UK. Got it?'

Alex left the kitchen. He ran across the patio and swerved between the trees; a branch of an oak caught him across his cheek. He banged on the caravan door. He heard the latch, pulled open the door and jumped in. He turned the key and checked each of the windows. Catrina, biting her thumb nail, watched him.

'Oh, Catrina. What to do? What to do?'

He stood close to her and she put her head on his chest; he rubbed her shoulder. She said something.

'Sorry?'

She looked up at him. 'Cinza? Cinza?'

'I know. No, I don't know.'

He saw his mobile phone on the couch. Damn. It needed charging.

'Catrina,' Alex looked at her, trying to find some Portuguese words.

'Catrina, *tarde,* later we will ...'

Her scream made him look up. At the window was Gordon and across his shoulder he balanced the lump hammer.

Minho Moments

*

Tumbling Stones

Malfalda raised her head. The reredos was beautiful; so large, the carved figures and flowers covered the whole of the chapel wall and the afternoon sunlight, coming through the door, lit the gilded woodwork.

As she moved to get more comfortable, her chair creaked; she rested back and felt the bars hard against her spine. She wriggled her toes to forestall the cramp in her calves which she knew would soon begin. Despite the sun, the chapel felt cold; it always was as it was only opened this one time of the year. She lifted her chin and moved the knot of her headscarf, then patted her chest to feel the filigree gold chains. The priest had been talking - talking for some time - she only seemed to be able to catch an odd word here and there - she put her hands together under her apron and closed her eyes. Mufflings brought her back from her dream. Chairs scraped on the stone floor and behind her *Senhora* Barbosa was complaining about something. It took time to get out of the chapel; this year there were even more immigrants than usual at the service and some late comers began crowding in. Malfalda stood in the aisle and watched one who was leaning against the altar while his wife took his photo; his elbow pushed against the vase of flamingo lilies rucking the lace edging of the altar cloth.

Outside the congregation huddled together waiting for the priest. He came out of the chapel following the acolyte who carried the silver crucifix high above his head. The procession began; some of the men slipped away to find a corner in the food tent for a game of cards. Malfalda kept her distance behind *Senhora* Barbosa. She did not want to hear any more about the ungrateful daughter-in-law or the problems with the gas bottle deliveries. The procession took the sandy path down through the pines to an open area and the stone cross. Everyone gathered around the priest whilst he prayed; Malfalda tried to listen, but somewhere high above, a bird was singing, then the priest said 'Amen' and procession returned to the chapel.

Mrs Palmer raised her head. The mountains were beautiful. Between the blurred greens of eucalyptus and pine, the granite chunks glinted in the sun.

Looking from the window, there was one or two of the hairpin bends she could have done without when the coach seemed to be ready to topple from the road down into the fern covered crevices. Before they reached the river, the driver had pulled over for the passengers to watch the wild horses; little family groups their coats the colour of buffed conkers; tails and mains a shaggy black. The surprise for everyone had been the boy appearing over the ridge; his horse a pale grey. He waved at the holidaymakers, then turning on the spot had galloped over the bridge, past the waterfall crashing white against the black wet rocks. The coach parked in the last space on the flat mossy area by the chapel railings. Mrs Palmer knew she it would be while before she got off. She closed her eyes letting the murmurings of the others deciding what to take and what to leave on the coach swirl around. Someone touched her arm, she opened her eyes. It was the nice young man with large ears. Poor thing, she thought every time she looked at him.

'May I help you?' he asked.

'That's kind, but the courier will collect me in a minute. You go on - there seems plenty to see.'

From the window she watched her holiday companions. Some had already walked past the railings through the gate towards the chapel; others were by the edge of the parking space looking down into the valley at the monastery; a rectangle of slate-coloured cells, surrounded by cork trees. Two keen photographers clambered over a boulder to get a better view of a herd of bullocks. Mrs Palmer knew she was the oldest and least active of the party, but the courier had been splendid and now she helped her from the coach, adjusted the bag across her shoulder and put the wheeled walking frame in front of her.

'Thank you my dear - you're so kind.'

'*Não é nada.* It's nothing. Just be careful of the uneven ground.'

Mrs Palmer walked slowly along the cobbles - the pain in her hip was bad today; once through the gate she wondered where she should go. She became aware of people behind her and moved away as a boy carrying a crucifix, followed by a priest and a procession passed her. Shouts, and a vehicle hooting, made her turn and coming from behind the chapel was an open truck packed with people. It bounced over the grass and stopped by the barbecues. Mrs Palmer noticed a trombone, its brass twinkling in the sun, and there was a man holding a drum above his head and a young girl dangling a trumpet over the tailboard.

The young man with the large ears touched her arm and pointed to a stone bench opposite the chapel door.

'I think you'll be safer over there.'

Mrs Palmer nodded. 'Yes, I think you are right.'

The stone bench was warm; the sun not too bright and the drifting breeze blew the smoke away the barbecues. The whiffs of cooked chicken made Mrs Palmer regret she had decided on only a salad for lunch.

Malfalda waited her turn. A narrow path encircled the chapel bordered by a low granite wall; the stones standing like a line of sentries. Around her people moved towards the path. As soon as there was a space Malfalda placed her hand on the wall for balance; the sharp edge sunk into her palm. As she bent her legs, she turned sideways and put her other hand on the top of the wall. This time she knew the stone had broken the skin. Once on her knees she took her hands from the wall and curled her fingers to stop the blood. The grit pressed into knees; she paused wanting the pain to subside. Her own private prayers ran through her mind and she began her penance. Someone nudged her shoulder; the queue was bunching up. Little stones fell from her knee as she lifted her leg; others were embedded in her skin. Malfalda squeezed shut her eyes, sucked in her bottom lip and began crawling along the path. When she opened her eyes she was at the corner of the chapel; the path had turned and widened out; she rested her fist against the wall. She looked across the valley to the distance mountains; their grey peaks pushing into the sky. The fire-break, a ribbon of brown divided the pine forest that ran down to a gully: the trees looked black in the deep shade. Someone whispered a rude word near her ear. She knew it was one of the immigrants. She stopped and straightened her headscarf. Let him wait. There was now a long gap between her and the person in front; she tried to move a little faster.

Malfalda, her knees numb, saw people standing up in front of her and knew she had reached the end of her journey. Hands pushed under her armpits and she was lifted up. Two neighbours walked with her to the food tent, in the entrance was a young boy holding a large accordion, only his head and legs visible. His fingers fluttered over the buttons; there was a breathy squeak and a tune swallowed up all the chatter and clatter of the *Festa*.

Mrs Palmer watched the last of the congregation go through to the food tent. The accordion was not her favourite instrument. She dragged her walking frame nearer and stood up. With her first step she blew out a soundless whistle; not the other hip as well? The chapel was empty. She stood at the altar, touched the blood red petals of the flamingo lilies and smoothed the lace edge of the cloth. The carved saints on the reredos looked down at her. She noticed Saint Paul's book, though the wood was chipped, it shone in bright vermilion; Saint John's scroll did seem out of proportion to his body, but cherubs and angels, leaves, flowers and garlands glowed in rich shining gold.

Out by the doorway Mrs Palmer squinted at the sun. A rainbow of colours spun past her as the folk dancing girls skipped their way up to the stage. Next came the men in black suits, their wide brimmed black hats tilted; scarlet cummerbunds wound tight around their white embroidered shirts.

Malfalda was sitting on the stone seat. Mrs Palmer walked across, smiled and sat down. She looked at Malfalda's necklaces, then touched her own blouse. Now what was the word for pretty? Every day of the holiday she had looked up a word or two in her phrase book in the hope to use them.

'*Bonito,*' she said.

Malfalda smiled; held the necklace closer for her to see. Hearts, like gold lace, swung on twisted chains; filigree medallions dangled from linked coils and gold ribbons were set with sapphire, ruby and amber stones. Malfalda lightly touched Mrs Palmer's hand. Mrs Palmer moved her fingers and the diamond in her engagement ring twinkled. She laid her hand on her blouse again, to indicate her heart. Malfalda nodded, and stretched out her hands. Mrs Palmer put her hands out as well and the two women looked at each other's wedding bands. Mrs Palmer compared the hands: both had knuckles too large, and veins standing up from the wrinkles. She looked at their nails, then folded her hands into her lap: her nails were like polished coral whereas Malfalda's were thick and jagged.

Next to the food tent, the band in their navy blue suits trimmed with maroon braid, and satisfied from their barbecued chicken and beer, crashed their music into the sky. Squashed in the tiny bandstand they began with melodies from musicals, switched to a little Mozart; the trombonist played a pop number as a solo piece; there was an aria from *Madam Butterfly* before the conductor gathered the musicians together for a finale of folk tunes.

Then the young man with the large ears was standing by the stone bench.

'Is it time we were making a move?' asked Mrs Palmer.

He held the walking frame steady as she pulled herself up.

Malfalda also stood, nodded a goodbye and, with other villagers, walked away through the gate.

The coach was stuffy, the armrest was hot to touch, her feet were beginning to swell and a fly ran up and down her window. The driver inched the coach between the dawdling crowds onto the road. Would downhill hairpin bends be worse than uphill ones? thought Mrs Palmer. She wasn't going to look out of the window, but when the coach slowed behind a bunch motor cyclists all riding three abreast, she glanced across at a small meadow; the grass a fresh green compared with the surrounding scrub and gorse. Dead branches woven into a fence encircled the meadow; a woman standing by the fence watched two grazing sheep. The braking of the coach made the woman look towards the road. As Mrs Palmer waved, her engagement ring clicked against the window and the fly disappeared.

Malfalda held up her hand and her necklaces glinted in the setting sun.

"Old women sit, stiffly, mosaics of pain...their memories: a heap of tumbling stones." - Babette Deutsch

*

Love Unreturned

The amber light was flashing: *"Proceed with Caution."* Jim spun the wheel quickly and his car crossed in front of the oncoming truck. He drove through the gate and circled around deciding on a bay in the empty car park. He left the car and went and bought tickets for the ferry. As he came out of the office he saw she had parked the Jag next to his car. She stood winding her scarf more tightly round her coat collar and lifted the ends over her head to make a hood. Jim opened his arms for her to snuggle against his duffel coat, but she turned and watched the ferry docking against the quay.

'Luiza my love - you're here. I thought ...'

'Let's have a coffee. I'm frozen.'

'We've only got a few minutes.'

'Plenty of time.'

He followed her across to the café as the first of the cars drove off the ferry and out into the town. Jim paid for the coffees and they took them outside. Luiza sipped her drink. Cars were arriving and queuing by the barrier. Jim finished his coffee and threw the carton in the bin.

'Come on - they'll be loading.'

'Last on, last off - what does it matter?'

Jim smiled, 'True.'

They walked to Jim's car; he opened the passenger door.

Luiza said: 'Think it better if we take both our cars.'

'What? That's a silly idea ...'

'No. I want to take my car as well. No time to argue.'

All the vehicles had driven onto the ferry. Jim got into his car, revved up the ramp and parked on the car deck. He looked in the rear view mirror as Luiza followed. Her car was last and then the crewman pulled across the safety chain and the ferry's engines shuddered as the vessel moved out into the river.

'Good you brought your scarf.'

Jim buttoned his coat at the neck. They were standing by the rail and the Portuguese town grew smaller by the minute. The wind dragged the river into foamy waves and the ferry rocked its way across to Galicia.

'Shall we sit up on top deck?'

Luiza ignored the question and Jim thought his words had been taken away by the wind. He put his arm around Luiza's shoulders and moved her towards the stairs.

'I'm cold. I'm going to sit in my car.'

Jim waited a few moments, then edged between the cars and climbed in beside her.

'I thought you wanted to be up on deck.'

'No. Not without you. Anyway we've got so much to talk about."

'Not now.' Luiza looked at her watch.

Jim said: 'Are you going to change the time?'

Luiza untucked her scarf, took a comb from her bag and pulled it through her hair; each time the strands straightened they bounced back. Jim wound a curl round his finger and gently tugged it.

He said again. 'Change the time Luiza. We'll have lost an hour together once we reach the other side.'

'It's not worth it. Have to alter it again once we come back.'

'Might not come back.'

Luiza looked at him.

'Now you are being silly. That's not going to happen.'

'You never know.'

A silence stayed in the car: eventually Luiza said:

'Look. We're nearly here. Better get back to your car.'

Luiza accelerated the Jag off the ferry, overtook Jim's car as they drove across the car park and took the narrow road up from the quay. Jim followed for a few minutes, then hooted, but Luiza didn't slow down. There was a lay-by ahead and Jim wanted to pull over and talk to her, but she drove on. Ahead

Jim saw the crossroads and indicated to turn right, but at the last moment had to carry on over to keep up with her. The car behind blasted its horn and Jim opened the window and waved his apology. Luiza suddenly took a sharp left and the car bumped down a dirt track; Jim followed wondering what her plan was. They were now several kilometres from the hotel going in the opposite direction. The track opened up into a narrow, shrub-lined road that Jim realised ended by a small harbour and beach. Luiza stopped by the sea wall and waited for him. He parked next to her, got out and opened her door.

'Well, this is a surprise. Wondered where you were taking me.'

Luiza didn't answer, but pulled her scarf up by her ears. Jim looked across the road; between a pharmacy and a bar was a restaurant; its torn sun canopy flapped over the door and a stack of chairs were chained to a metal post.

'A fish restaurant? Yes, fine, but I thought we were going to the hotel for lunch and then maybe stay ...'

Jim hurried after Luiza as she crossed to the restaurant; inside it smelt not only of fish, but of damp. A woman was bending by an empty grate.

Luiza went straight to a table and sat down. Jim began to unbutton his coat, then changed his mind.

'Is she going to light the fire?' he asked.

Luiza didn't reply. Jim sat down, looked first for the *The Dish of the Day* sign, then across at the other tables.

'Where's a menu?'

Luiza shrugged.

'Well, I think I'll have *leguado*.'

'Sole?" Luiza shook her head, 'They won't have that.'

'What about *dorada*?'

Luiza laughed: 'Sea bass? I don't think so.'

As the woman moved away from the grate one of her slippers fell off: she left it on the floor.

'We'll have the *pulpo*.' called Luiza

'No. Luiza - I hate octopus you know that.'

'Don't think there's anything else.'

'Then why are we here in this ...' Jim glanced round. 'Just exactly why are we here?'

Luiza got up and followed the woman to the kitchen door. Jim could only hear the odd word: "later" then "no trouble". A waiter brought a basket of bread. Jim took a slice, felt the dry surface and dropped it back in the basket.

What is this all about? This isn't what I planned, he thought. Is all this going to unravel? No it can't - Not now. No Luiza. No.

Jim moved the oil bottle; it left a yellow circle on the paper; he put it back. He needed Luiza. These last few weeks had been so new and fresh. Life, he had to admit, had been lonely at times ... always difficult for an ex-pat on his own, especially one who didn't play golf. Work kept him busy, but everyone needed that something extra. The boys had got their own lives ... good jobs in Scotland ... anyway their mother had soured anything they might have had ... but that day ... meeting Luiza.

Luiza came back to the table. 'I've ordered rice, or do you want boiled potatoes?'

'What will make it taste better?' Jim smiled at his joke, but Luiza called out:

'Yes, Rice.'

'Right. Let's have some wine.'

'No. Water will do.'

The waiter must have heard, as a moment later he brought a small bottle of water and two glasses.

'Oh, come on Luiza. What is it? Have I done something wrong. Upset you?'

'No. No. Of course not.'

Luiza poured out the water. Jim lifted his glass then put it down and caught hold of her hand.

'Luiza.' He spoke her name slowly.

She pulled her hand away as the waiter put a dish of rice between them. She spooned some rice onto her plate. The waiter returned with the octopus stew. Jim sighed.

'Don't make a fuss.'

Luiza put some rice on his plate, then with a fork hooked a piece of octopus and dropped it on to of the rice.

'I don't want much. God, it looks vile.'

Luiza ignored him, served herself and began eating. Jim moved the food around, looking for something he hoped he could chew, then swallow. Luiza had two helpings then put her fork down and waved to the waiter to clear away the plates. The waiter hesitated by the side of Jim.

'Yes, Yes. Finished. *Gracias*,' said Jim.

'Dessert?' The waiter asked.

'Not for me, but an espresso please.'

Luiza shook her head.

'Nothing,' then looked past Jim as the restaurant door opened. The two men let the door slam with the wind, dragged chairs from another table and sat down by Luiza. Jim looked at her, then the men.

'Yes?'

'A very good afternoon Jim.'

The man's accent rolled the words into one.

'Luiza ... ?'

Jim wanted her to look at him, but she was folding her napkin into a fan and took no notice. The man shrugged his coat from his shoulders and clicked his fingers at the waiter.

'*Aguardiente* for all.' He circled his hand over the table.

'Not for me ....'

'Jim, Jim, let's be sociable.'

'Who the hell are you?'

The other man was filling his pipe and said:

'We're friends of Luiza.'

And you're from Liverpool, thought Jim.

'Luiza. What is going on?'

This doesn't really concern Luiza now.'

'I'll say it again. Who are you?'

The man pointed his pipe.

'That is Chico and I'm Dave.

'Well, Chico and Dave, piss off.'

The bark in Jim's voice made the waiter take a step back from the table. Chico reached over and took the bottle from the tray and as the waiter put down the four glasses he filled each one to the brim. He lifted his drink.

'Bottoms Up,' he said, then smacked the empty glass back on the table. Luiza fingered the stem of her glass but did not pick it up. Dave finished his drink and went out of the restaurant. Jim turned round; he could see him sheltering by the stacked chairs.

'So Jim,' Chico shifted and his thighs resettled over the chair.

'How's business?'

Jim didn't reply; he looked at Luiza, but she just stared at her glass. He turned to Chico:

'I don't know who you are … I don't care who you are, but you do understand English? Yes? Well, piss off.'

'Luiza,' Chico pulled his coat over his shoulders, stood up, jerked his head, 'Outside.'

'Luiza, you don't have ...' but she jumped up and followed him. Jim took a sip of the spirit, waited the three, four seconds before the burning filled his mouth then gulped. What the hell's going on? He went to the window and watched the three of them; they had moved over to the sea wall and were standing between his car and the Jag. This whole day has gone crazy. How does she know these clowns?

The old woman came grumbling out of the kitchen and waited by the till. Jim calculated the cost of the meal, added on another ten Euros, laid the money on the table and smiled a 'Thanks' to the woman; though heaven knows why he thought, and stepped out into the cold grey of the late afternoon.

The wind was whipping across the harbour and Chico clasping his coat to his chest trotted past Jim's car and climbed into a Range Rover. As Jim got closer to the cars, Dave came to meet him.

'Let's go and have a coffee.'

'No. I don't want a coffee. What I want is for you to disappear and I want to talk to Luiza. Luiza?'

He tried to side step round Dave, but he barred his way.

'No. No. Jim. Luiza's going to have a chat with Chico and I'm going to have a chat with you.'

Luiza had got into the Range Rover. Dave pressed the stem of his pipe into Jim's ribs. For one horrible moment Jim looked at it as though it was a gun. I'm going mad, he thought.

'Okay. We'll have a coffee, then Luiza and I are leaving and whatever game this is, can come to an end.'

The bar was as cold and damp as the restaurant. Jim scuffed away cigarette butts and empty screwed up sugar packets as he stood by the counter. Dave ordered two coffees; the girl, a lollipop stuck in her mouth, served him while watching a soap on the television that was fixed above the coffee machine.

At the table Jim pushed his coffee away and said:

'Out with it. This is Maggie's doing, isn't it?'

'Who's Maggie?'

'My ex-wife.'

'Nah, this is nothing personal. This is business.'

'Business? My business is perfectly fine. And nothing to do with you.'

'Yes,' Dave emptied three packets of sugar into his coffee, 'It is fine and you want it to continue?'

A feeling of apprehension started to squeeze in amongst the irritation and anger of the day. Dave stirred his coffee, then tapped the table with the spoon.

'The holiday trade. Old biddies enjoying coach trips to see the sights. Energetic walkers trampling over the countryside. You wouldn't want that to end now would you Jim?'

Jim stood up.

'Sit down and listen. You make two trips to Porto every week.'

'So? Nothing to do with you.'

'Just shut up. In the dash of your car is a package. Tomorrow you will go to Porto and take the package.'

Jim leaned over the table, 'I'm not taking any package anywhere.'

He walked towards the door.

'Pity. Luiza said you would.'

Jim turned back to the table.

'What's she got to do with all this?'

'Ask her. Let's go.'

He clattered the cup back onto the saucer.

'This coffee is disgusting,' he shouted to the girl.

The girl picked up the remote control and increased the volume on the television.

Outside Chico was in the Range Rover and Luiza, hunched up by the wall was watching a fishing boat rolling towards the harbour. Chico leaned out of his window.

'Everything all right Jim?' His laugh ended in a wheeze of coughing. Dave got into the passenger seat, the Range Rover reversed into the road and powered away.

Jim opened the passenger door of his car.

'Get in.'

Luiza pushed herself away from the wall. In the car Jim pulled down the dash. A package, the shape and size of a paperback book was wedged on top of his binoculars. Luiza stood by the open door.

'Luiza. Get in.'

She sat in the seat, elbows on knees, her chin resting in her hands.

Jim said: 'I'm lost for words. Absolutely lost for words. Is this what it's all been about?'

She didn't move.

'Is it? Is it? Just you with some sordid little plan. All your talk about us. Us? There never was any us was there?'

He thought he saw her shake a head.

'It's not going to happen. Taking packages to Porto! God! How stupid do you think I am?'

Luiza dropped her hands and looked at him.

'Please Jim. Do it ...'

'No!' The word bounced off the windscreen. He turned the ignition key, pulled at his seatbelt, stretched his arm across her lap and opened the door.

'I believe your car ... your Jag ... the car you begged for ... and I bought for you ... is parked just there.'

He hated the sarcasm in his voice, but he couldn't think how else to talk to her. Any other tone would have had him swearing at her, or even worse crying, holding her close, and saying he would make everything okay. She got out and slammed the door; he hit the accelerator.

He drove on to the cross-roads, pulled over and waited. He had parked opposite a farmyard; a cat huddled by the gate; he could hear dog a barking. Next to the farm wall were two persimmon trees; their orange fruit hanging from the bare branches like Christmas lanterns.

Christmas. Two months ago when he had first met Luiza. Christmas in Portugal - a brisk enjoyable occasion. Plenty of food on Christmas Eve then Midnight Mass if you wish. Christmas Day watching a football match or at the café with the family. Next day it's back to work. It was on Christmas Eve that he decided to give himself a treat and book himself into the Castelo Hotel. He took the coastal road and in the bright winter sunshine the Atlantic waves crashed navy blue over the shore rocks; the water changing to turquoise as it sloshed and ebbed away in a white foam. At each bend in the road, Jim glanced out at sea; and its the energy delighted him; the spray flying high into air then falling like rain.

The hotel, balanced on a rocky outcrop, resembled a medieval fortress and its suits of armour, wide staircase and carved oak chests in the foyer suited his mood. He promised himself a 5 star brandy after his evening meal. He noticed her as he stood by the Reception Desk. She had been moving newspapers from a sofa, then picked up a cushion; the gold brocade emphasised her black suit. It was when he was sitting on the covered terrace, enjoying his brandy that he saw her again. She paused by his chair, wished him a good evening, then hesitated. He asked her to join him, immediately thought it a foolish idea if she was on duty, but she agreed. He loved the way she drank her lemonade; sucking the straw and making silly gurgling noises to catch the very last drop at the bottom of the glass. And they talked and talked, or rather he talked and she listened. About his boys, his ex-wife, his op on his knee, transferring his travel business to Portugal, his love of Portugal, his time as Chairman of the tennis club in Kent. How he had difficulty understanding the Portuguese when they spoke too quickly. He talked and she listened.

'Sorry, you must be completely bored. Another drink? Something stronger?'

'No, no,' she laughed, 'I must go.' She stepped away from the table then turned.

'Your room is to your liking?'

'Yes. Marvellous sea views.'

'It's number …?'

'Seventeen.'

'Yes, of course. Goodnight.'

Jim was pleased with himself; he had unpacked his case completely; taken his washing gear into the bathroom and laid it out properly on the glass shelf and had even hung up his jacket. There was a tap on the door; he was about to call out when it opened and she stood there holding the champagne and two glasses.

'What's this? Christmas Greetings from the Management?'

She shook her head.

'No. From me.'

Her long skirt floated into an arc of green as she turned and kicked the door shut.

Jim looked into the wing mirror. Luiza came and parked behind him. He got out of the car and waited; she wound down her window and tried to hand him a piece of paper.

'This is the number you have to ring.'

'Do you not get it Luiza. It is not going to happen.'
'Jim, plea ...'
He thumped the roof of the Jag. 'Bitch.'

There were not many vehicles driving on to the ferry. Jim followed a minibus and once parked, got out and stood by the rail waiting; his chest hammering. The crewman was ready with the safety chain when the Jag sped across the quay. Someone shouted, the man flapped his arms impatiently and the ramp was dragged in as soon as Luiza drove on to the deck; the ferry edged out into the river.

Jim pushed behind the minibus and climbed up onto the open top deck. He walked to the stern pulled his hood up and looked over the rail at the river. Bubbles of scum churned to the surface in the khaki coloured water. From his pocket he took his key ring and found the penknife and slit open the package – inside were dozens of small white packets. He looked over his shoulder. The fine rain had put off anyone wanting to come up on deck. He dropped a packet over the side. It floated on the water, following the ferry. He looked round on the deck again, but when he glanced down, the packet had sunk. One after the other he tossed the packets into the river. Finally, he screwed up the wrapper and flung it out as far as he could. He brushed his palms and walked towards the stairs. Standing two steps down was Luiza. She stared at him then tried to pass; he caught hold of her arm.

'Luiza. It will be all right.'

'Go away,' she dragged herself from him and walked along the deck.

Jim followed, 'Luiza.'

The ferry chugged on towards land; Jim could make out the clock face on the church spire.

'Luiza.'

She reached the stern and continued round the deck to the other side of the ferry. Jim went back down the stairs and waited by her car. People were getting back in their vehicles. Jim ran up the stairs and walked quickly round the top deck; she wasn't there. Near the bow was the W.C. It was engaged; he waited, but when the door opened, out came the driver of the minibus.

'*Todo seu* – All yours,' he grinned.

Jim heard a car horn. The ferry had docked and the ramp was down. Vehicles were driving off; the minibus had left and his car was next. He drove across the car park, out through the gates and parked by the side of the road. He could see the Jag still on the deck. Then two of the crew, trying to open an umbrella, hurried from the ferry over to the office. A minute later a man in uniform followed them back to the ferry. Jim got out of the car and stood by the metal fence trying to get a better view. Another man in uniform appeared from the office talking on a mobile phone. Four men, pulling on waterproofs, came out of a hut; they climbed down steps from the quay into a dinghy. The dinghy bobbed behind the ferry's hull. Jim ran over to the car park gate, but the man with the mobile held up his palm to stop him. Jim could see the dinghy being rowed away from the ferry. One man crouched over the gunwale; the beam of his torch shone on the water. Jim heard the police sirens; a convey of Jeeps came from the town centre; the traffic light was flashing amber: *Proceed with Caution.* The Jeeps swept across the junction; a taxi swerved.

From the river's estuary lightning forked, and the drab, wet sky lit up. At that moment Jim looked again at the ferry. In the sudden brightness, the ruby red Jag dazzled like the first colour in a spectrum after a storm.

"Let no one who loves be called altogether unhappy. Even love unreturned has its rainbow." J M Barrie.

*

Cafe Violeta

'*Nao! Nao!* Not again!'
Senhor Moreira banged his fist on the counter.
'*Nao!*'
Throwing the tea towel over the coffee machine he pushed between the tables. Just as he reached the café door, it swung open.
'I'm so sorry,'
Moreira rubbed his shoulder.
'It nothing; *nada.*'
The girl again said: 'I'm sorry, but the door sticks a bit.'
'Eh?' He didn't seem to understand or be listening. He stepped out onto the pavement. Look at it! Third time this week. He watched as the suitcases and holdalls were being stacked around his chairs. One suitcase, an ugly shade of puce, had even been put on a table.
'Oi,' he pushed into the crowd. Some were congregated at the coach's door; others shuffling around looking for their luggage. The driver, checking a clipboard, ignored him. Moreira ran across the road and took the steps of the Hotel Boavista two at a time. In the

foyer the Receptionist looked up at the ping of the bell.

'*Senhor* Moreira? What's the matter? Are you ill?' Moreira tried to breath.

'Again ... and again ... and again ....'

'Please, *Senhor* Moreira do not point your finger like that at me. Now slowly tell me what is wrong.'

Moreira spluttered out his anger.

'Another coach. Blocking out all the sunlight. My café practically in darkness. And the luggage,' Moreira waved his arms in the air, 'Everywhere.'

His chest rose and he coughed out the words:

'Even on one of my tables.'

The swish of revolving doors caught the Receptionist's attention.

'Please, one moment *Senhor*." She moved away from him and unhooked a key from the wall. She handed the key to the Porter.

'Room Twenty Three. English *Senhora*'

Moreira turned and bolted out of the hotel; a taxi hooted.

'Hey Moreira; have you had enough of life?' shouted the driver.

Moreira jumped the kerb and onto the pavement, pushed one of the cases out of his way with his foot and went into the café. Look at it. No customers. So dark he could hardly see. Ah, yes in the corner. Was it the girl? Had she been served?

'Tomas,' he shouted.

The bead curtain rattled and the waiter appeared from the kitchen. Moreira nodded his head towards the corner of the café.

'Don't sigh,' he said as Tomas walked past him, 'And always take a tray with you.'

Tomas watched the café owner pick up the tea towel, give the coffee machine a quick polish and go back through to the kitchen. Tomas sauntered over to the girl.

'*Sim*?'

'A coffee with milk, please.'

Tomas, behind the counter, as he began preparing the coffee, looked over his shoulder at the girl. She had lifted her rucksack onto her lap and taken out, what Tomas guessed, was a travel guide. She flicked through the pages. Tomas watched as she leaned over the book. Her hair ... what colour would he call it ... *mel* ?... honey? swung forward and hid her face. He noticed how the rims of her ears peeped through strands of the hair.

The hot milk bubbled over and he yelped. Moreira shouted through the beads.

'What's going on?'

Tomas wiped up the milk and set out a clean saucer. He was carrying the coffee across to the table, when he remembered his boss's words, so he took the coffee back to the counter, placed it on a tray and started across the café again. As he reached the table the coffee cup and saucer began to slide. He saved it just in time and put the drink by the side of the travel book. The girl didn't look up; she had taken a sketch pad from her rucksack. Tomas went back behind the counter and watched her hand as she took a sachet of sugar from the dish. He marvelled at her precise tearing of the corner of the paper. Her fingers were thin and white. She stirred her coffee; little finger bent. She then first put a finger to her lips, pressed up the spilt sugar grains, sucked her finger, and wiped it dry on her jeans. Tomas set out more saucers on the counter. He looked again; she was texting on her mobile. Outside the coach's engine began to rev and slowly it moved along the street. The sudden brightness in the café made the girl look about her. She saw Tomas and smiled; he smiled back.

Senhor Moreira came out from the kitchen, opened the café door and glanced up and down the street. The coach was turning onto the Promenade car-park. Moreira walked about the pavement, tidying his tables and chairs. Back in the café, the girl slid on the rucksack, spilled some coins onto the table and moved them around, setting out the exact money. Moreira stood by the counter.

'All Okay?' he called.

The girl nodded and headed for the door. Tomas reached the door before her and pulled it open.

'It st-e-e-e-ks,' he said.

The girl smiled an agreement.

Moreira couldn't believe that the next day was an exact replay. Middle of the afternoon, just as the sun was reaching over from the sea-front into the Rua de Bandeira and tourists taking a stroll away from the beach looking for coffee and cake there was the coach – right outside Café Violeta.

'Tomas. You're in charge.'

Moreira untied his apron and took his jacket from the door hook.

'Never mind the Receptionist; I'm going to speak to the Manager.'

Tomas was leaning on the counter reading a football magazine when he heard the door open and the girl walk in and sit at a table.

'*Café com leite?*' he asked.

'Café? Sorry? ... Yes, coffee with milk. Thank you.'

The girl opened and pulled out the sketch pad and mobile from her rucksack. Tomas turned from the counter and called:

'*Bolos?*'

'Sorry?'

'*Bolos.* Cakes.'

He waved his hand over a group of cake stands. The girl came to the counter and leaned her elbows on the polished wood. Tomas lifted the cover from one of the stands.

'*Pastel de Nata*,' he said.

Little tartlets, the baked egg custard centres shining with burnished cinnamon, were piled into a pyramid.

'Mmm...' The girl looked at the other stands. Tomas took off another cover.

'*Tarte de Amêndoa*.'

Caramelised bronze almonds lay in a large crust of flaky pastry. With a flourish he lifted the lid of the last stand. Squashed together were oval dough balls fried to a crisp gold and covered in sugar that was coarse and glittering; from the centre of each one oozed rich amber custard. The girl shook her head and Tomas drooped his shoulders in comic disappointment. The girl laughed and then pointed.

'*Bolos de Berlim*,' said Tomas taking tongs from a mahogany drawer and putting the cake with a paper napkin on a plate.

The girl went back to the table and texted a message. Tomas put the plate on a tray and carefully carried it over to the table. The girl put down her phone and wrapped the napkin around the cake; she bit into the crunchy, sweet dough. Tomas went back to the counter and folded away his magazine. He looked at the girl; with the second bite the custard trickled down her chin; she giggled and as she wiped her mouth, the custard ran down her hand and dripped onto the table. Tomas brought more napkins, but the paper shredded and stuck both to her palms and the table. Tomas ran behind the counter and came with a damp cloth and towel.

The girl shook her head.

'Thank you. Thank you. I'm so silly.'

'*O quê?*' Tomas asked as the door swung open and Moreira, pulling off his jacket, ignored both the waiter and girl strode across to the kitchen.

'Tomas – come here.'

Tomas stood waiting; Moreira, putting on his apron, pulled and broke one of the strings. Tomas went back into the café; the girl had gone, but on the table was a five Euro note.

Despite it being overcast, the following day, for Moreira, was a happier one; even the ten minutes of light drizzle that swept along the Rua de Bandeira brought in more customers than he expected - and no coach parked in front of the Café Violeta. Tomas noticed the girl did not come to the café.

It was the next day: Moreira fidgeted the cake stands into a regimented line; then the square of sun shining on the tiled floor disappeared as a coach stopped outside the café. Moreira swore.

'Right. Never mind the Receptionist; forget the idiot of a Manager, I'm going to have a word – no – I'm going to have several words with the owner of that Hotel Boavista.' Moreira pushed his face against the window.

'Look at them; even sitting at my tables.'

Tomas sauntered around the café checking the sugar bowls.

Moreira took off his apron and threw it at Tomas.

'Fetch my jacket.'

The café door crashed behind Moreira. Just as Tomas turned the sign that had swung to *CLOSED* back to *OPEN*, the girl appeared.

Tomas began making the coffee; the girl sat the table texting; she looked up and nodded an agreement for the drink. Tomas brought the coffee, then pointed towards at one of the cake stands.

'*Bolo*?'

'Yes please.'

Tomas put the plate with the little tartlet and a napkin on the table, gave a little bow and said:

'*Para voce - Pastel de Nata.*'

He then held up a finger, went and ducked down behind the counter and brought to the table a bundle of paper napkins. The girl laughed. Tomas, as he stacked clean cups and saucer watched her: first the sugar in the coffee; the stirring; licking the spoon clean. A small bite from the tartlet; a crumb stuck to her lip; the tip of her tongue searched for it. Then a taste of coffee; another bite; checking her phone; finishing the tartlet and brushing her mouth with the napkin. She leant back in her chair, looked up at the ceiling and watched the creaking fan while slowly sip by sip finished her coffee.

Tomas knew that his boss's meeting with the owner of Hotel Boavista had not been a success when the door opened and Moreira stumped in. Tomas caught the beads as they bounced over the kitchen doorway and explained about the five Euro note. Moreira went to the till, calculated and slapped the bill down on the girl's table. She fished for the correct money from her jeans' pocket, picked up her phone and rucksack and put the money on the counter. It was when he heard the café door close that Tomas, still in the kitchen, realised she had left.

'The police. I'm fetching the police.'

'*Senhor*, No, you can't .... I mean, it will cause trouble.'

'Trouble? Don't you think I've had enough trouble already?'

'But *Senhor*, it's only for half an hour.'

'Half an hour is half an hour of rubbishy cases and bags outside my café.' Moreira caught hold of the door handle, 'Have you unpacked the box of Vinho Verde?'

'No but ...'

'Just do it,' and Moreira, still wearing his apron, left the café.

Tomas was lining up the last of the slender green bottles on the shelf when the girl came in.

'*Boa tarde.* Coffee with milk?'

'Good afternoon. Yes please.'

The girl sat at the table tossing her mobile phone from one hand to another; she then began flicking through the pages of her travel book. Tomas brought her the coffee.

'Thank you.'

Tomas stood by the window: he could hear Moreira, the coach driver and the policeman all talking at once. He walked over to the counter and coughed - the girl looked up and saw he was holding two of the cake covers above his head like a pair of cymbals. The girl giggled.

'Okay.'

Tomas cut into the tart, and by the side of the wedge of caramelised almonds, put a fork, a napkin then waited. The girl was studying a map in the book; today she had a hair tied up with a white ribbon. He served her the tart. Using the side of the fork, she broke off a triangle and stabbed it, then lifted to her mouth; it fell first onto the front of her tee-shirt then the floor. She prised off one, two, three toasted almonds to eat, then lifted the flan between her thumb and finger and bit into it. When Tomas returned with a dustpan and brush, there was shouting outside, then the café door opened, closed, opened again and as Moreira, followed by the policeman came in, the coach drove away.

The policeman pulled out a chair and sat down. Moreira poured out a brandy and took it to the table. The girl re-packed her rucksack and settled her bill with Moreira. Tomas reached the door before her.

'It st-e-e-e-k-s,' he said.

Moreira had sat down with the policeman:

'Tomas, bring the bottle.'

The girl smiled at Tomas.

'Thank you and Goodbye.'

Tomas edged between the tables and chairs; he caught one or two words between laughter and glasses clinking. Eventually the policeman stood, stretched his arms, winked at Tomas, punched Moreira lightly on the chest and left.

'All sorted.'

'*Senhor*?'

'All sorted. In future all coaches will have to park further down Rua de Bandeira - past the zebra crossing.'

'That'll be outside the *Café Doce*.'

Moreira shrugged and poured himself another brandy.

As Ellen walked along the Rua de Banderia her mobile rang.

'You!' she cried, 'At last! Where have you been? What? Where? All right. I'll be there in two minutes.'

Ellen turned onto the Promenade, climbed over the sea wall and jumped down onto the beach. Atlantic rollers were bringing in the surfers on each wave.

'Hi, I'm here.'

A head popped up from behind a clump of marram grass.

Ellen dropped her rucksack and fell onto her knees.

'Becky. Where have you been?'

'Sorry. Sorry. Sorry.'

'Not good enough.'

'But you know I can't resist an Australian. Not one as gorgeous as ... Oh, he was perfect.'

'You didn't even text.'

'No time.'

'Don't be stupid,' Ellen pulled her tee-shirt over her head and using it as a pillow stretched out on the sand.

'Anyway," said Becky unwrapping a piece of chewing gum, 'What have you been doing?'

'Waiting for you.'

'No seriously. Been sketching?'

'Yes ... you know I still want half the rent for the apartment. And we leave tomorrow.'

'I know.'

Ellen sat up and took her sketch pad from her rucksack and handed to Becky. Becky turned each page.

'These are great. They really are.'

'Thanks. Anyway, you know we're getting the first train to Porto, so it's an early night.'

'Yes, yes. I see most of your sketches are of the fishing harbour and the fort. And is this the Main Street?

'Yes - Rua de Banderia.'

Becky continued: 'All scenes around here. Didn't you go anywhere else?'

'No not really.'

'Ellen! Come on. Tell Aunty Becky.'

'Nothing to tell.'

Becky fell back on the sand and waved her legs in the air, 'Ell-en, Ell-en,' she sang, 'What's his name?'

Ellen didn't reply; she pushed some sand together, pulled at a blade of marram grass and stuck it on top of the little white mound. She made another little castle and another then said: 'Tomas.'

'Tomas,' *Senhor* Moreira brushed his hand over a table, 'Stop staring out of the window.'

Tomas opened the cafe door, stood on the pavement and looked up and down Rua de Banderia. A coach was parked just past the zebra crossing. Moreira followed him out, and opened the sun shades.

'You know, I have a feeling it's going to be a good day.'

Tomas didn't reply, but turned to go back into the café.

'What's the matter, my boy?'

Tomas looked back at Moreira.

Moriera laughed, 'Never mind.'

Tomas went into the café and looked at the row of cake stands.

'My *bolo* girl. I loved you.'

*

Raimund And Josefina

Raimund jumped to the side; just missed him. He turned; another one was coming up on his right. He moved away and waited for the line of passengers to pass. Damn wheely cases. Once he was in the railway's main vestibule he put down his own holdall. He looked up at the clock set in the glass arched windows, then heard a scuffling, turned and saw a woman trying to regain her balance. He grabbed up his holdall.

'I am so sorry ...'

The woman stared at him for a moment, re-hooked her bag on her shoulder and walked away.

'I say,' called Raimund, but she was lost in a bunch of giggling students.

Raimund stood on the pavement; the noise and smell and colour of the city churned about him. From between the queues of cars, that edged and squeezed for advantage, fumes rose up and hung in the hot day. It seemed out of boredom every driver was sounding the horn. People walking alone became enmeshed with others; couples weaved through chattering groups;

everyone's summer clothes reminded Raimund of a twisting kaleidoscope. In the middle of the road, the sun shone wildly on the roof of a car - its lime green sparkled and Raimund stepped into the gutter, threw his arm in the air and the taxi shoved up to the kerb and stopped a few steps away. Raimund turned to pick up his holdall as two young men moved towards the taxi, but he beat them to the door and threw himself on the hot leather. The taxi revved and jerked back into the jousting traffic. Raimund, feeling a little guilty, turned and looked out of the rear window at the men still by the kerb. A woman stepped into the road behind the taxi. Raimund watched her hesitate, then at a run, make it across.

'Stop!' his fist hit the back of the driver's seat.

'Eh?' The driver turned and frowned.

He thumped the seat again, 'Stop.'

Raimund looked again through the rear window. As the woman changed her bag from one shoulder to the other, the years evaporated.

***

Raimund looked again through the rear window. The girl changed her bag from one shoulder to the other. The chain on the handcuff was pulled and Raimund was dragged across the seat and fell onto the van's floor. There were two other men in the vehicle; friends from university, but they all ignored each other's gaze as the van bumped over cobbled streets, swerved and turned. After five - ten minutes Raimund realised they must have left the town, the road's surface was now smooth and the van increased it speed.

Raimund couldn't remember everything, but he remembered the long corridor; the guards' boots scraping the stone floor. His need to stride quickly feeling the fists push, pushing into his spine. He remembered how Alfonso or was it Julio nudged him and he looked behind to see how many more guards there were and when he turned back, another uniformed group waiting for them. The fusion of horror and rage as their trousers were pulled down: he had looked at Julio's pale and skinny legs; he could hear the guards' guffaws and he remembered thinking are they going to force us to shuffle down the corridor with our trousers round our ankles? Later the questions; questions he could not answer, then hours alone shivering and hungry. Next, suggestions followed by sniggering outside the cell. Then innuendos with stupid conclusions, that he wished he was brave enough to sneer at. He remembered saying:

'Where is he?' He was surprised at his courage.

The guard walked slowly around his chair even stepping over Raimund's out stretched legs. The lolling whilst being interrogated had been an idea he thought up; now he wasn't so sure it had been a good plan. He held his breath waiting for the smack across the head.

'Who?'

Raimund pushed himself up on the chair, lifted his chin and said, 'Julio.'

'Julio?'

The guard gave a tut. 'Julio who?'

'Julio Texeira.'

The guard patted his breast pockets then pulled out a packet of cigarettes. Raimund decided he would take one if offered, but the guard threw the packet on the table.

'Julio Texeira,' he spoke the words softly, almost hummed them, 'Is not here.'

Raimund didn't speak; he hoped his silence would make the guard continue. Some minutes went by. Raimund had tried several times counting the seconds, then, unable to keep the words in his mouth, shouted, 'Where is he, you bastard? What have you done to him?'

The guard lifted his fist and Raimund tensed waiting for the pain, but before it came he heard the guard whisper, 'I expect little Julio, little snivelling Julio, is now in heaven.'

***

Josefina watched the taxi speed away. A man's face appeared at the rear window; it turned away for second and then she saw him look again and the years evaporated.

***

Josefina watched the van speed away; she saw Raimund's face at the rear window, then he was gone. She remembered changing her bag of text books from one shoulder to the other. They had all been sitting at a table on the pavement. It was the table with the uneven leg and Julio had torn a page from his notebook to make a wedge. They had all put their hands on the table and cheered when it didn't rock. She remembered going inside the café to choose a cake, looking out through the open door and seeing the police van. As she stepped towards the door, the café owner had pulled her back and pushed her into a chair between an elderly couple; she remembered they were drinking hot chocolate.

She heard the one, two, three doors slam and ran out onto the pavement. She remembered picking up her bag that was still on her chair and then watching the van drive away.

She remembered how her father had looked over the top of his newspaper.

'I told you, time and again, to keep away from him. Communist agitator.'

'No, it's not like that. Raimund said we must fight against injust...'

'Fight! What kind of talk is that?'

'Raimund says ...'

Her father folded the paper and tossed it on to the table.

'That's enough. You're going to Aunt Rita's.'

'Aunt Rita! But she's in France.'

'Exactly. And that's where you are going. '

'But mother wouldn't want me to ...'

'I've decided, and you're going to tomorrow.'

'But father ... my studies ... my art ... you know I want ...'

'It's all arranged. You are going away from here and away from trouble.'

'Father, please no. Please.'

Josefina watched her father walk out onto the verandah and knock his pipe against the railings.

'Aunt Rita will find you work - there's plenty at the hotels.'

***

Raimund tapped the driver on the shoulder.

'Sorry about this.'

He got out of the taxi and waved to the two young men; they ran along the pavement and jumped into the car.

'Thanks mate.'

At first Raimund couldn't see the woman but then she was there talking on her mobile. He thought there was never going to be a gap in the traffic, but a car with a UK number plate slowed all the vehicles and he crossed the road. She didn't notice him until he was by her side.

'Josefina.'

She ended the call, but didn't speak.

'Josefina. It is you, isn't it?'

'Raimund? Rai – mund!'

'I thought it was you at the station, but then thought: no, can't be.'

'I can't believe this. I just can't. Raimund! I don't know whether to laugh or cry.'

'Look,' Raimund took her hand, 'Where are you going? Are you busy? We must talk. Let's go and laugh and cry over a coffee.'

Josefina looked at her watch. 'I'm meeting a friend at six. Going to the new Art Exhibition. We've got tickets.'

'Then we've got time. You won't be late for him.'

Josefina prodded Raimund's jacket.

'The friend is Claire; she's an American.'

'Good,' said Raimund.

'You've time for another coffee, or shall we have an aperitif?'

'Aperitif would be lovely. Back in a moment.'

Raimund watched her walk across the café to the cloakroom. Her story, she said was simple. After his arrest, her father had sent her to work in France. She had met a Portuguese boy, married him and both had stayed working in France. She'd had two children: a boy now working in California and the girl married to a Frenchman. She'd been widowed for seven years ago and was now living in a village a few miles from Porto. No, she had never continued with her art studies.

'That's a great pity,' said Raimund. 'Why not take it up now?'

Josefina laughed, 'Too many grey hairs.'

They lifted their drinks and both said: '*Saude*!'

Josefina speared an olive, 'Now you.'

Raimund rubbed his palm across his beard and thought how much shall I tell?

'After I got out,' he paused. 'Josefina.'

'Raimund. It's me you are talking to.'

'Yes,' he touched her hand, 'After I got out, I went to Brazil. Studied there. Got my engineering degree. Worked there for the next thirty – thirty five years...' The words fell over each other.

'And now you are back?'

'Yes. For good.'

'Did you ever find out who were the *bufos*?'

Raimund sighed. 'Who were the informers? The snitches? No. Everything is played close to the chest with the PIDE.'

'Raimund.'

'Never married by the way.'

'No?'

Raimund sighed, 'Couldn't find a girl like you.'

'Come on. In Brazil. All those beauties.'

'Plenty of girlfriends, I admit, but no one like you.'

'Raimund,' she made her voice severe, but then smiled and they both laughed. She looked at her watch.

'I've got to go.'

'We've got to meet again'

'Yes, of course. I'd like that.'

'This time next week?'

'Definitely. At São Bento Station?'

Raimund was half an hour early. He sauntered around the vestibule studying the tiles; the *azulegos* told the stories of Portugal's past. Not all its past he thought. He tried to remember his school history lessons: The Battle of Valdevez, the Conquest of Ceuta, but he liked the simple images of the oxen standing in the stream by the watermill; the smiling girls in national dress. He looked up at the clock. She was late. After another quarter of an hour, he thought she may not come. Another quarter of hour passed and he knew she was not going to come. A young girl, perched on a stool, was sketching the Valdevez battle; she saw him glance at the scene and leaned away for him to look closer at the sketch.

'Thank you,' he said and she grinned. He didn't want to go back to his apartment. He felt a fool for not getting her mobile number, or not giving her his. He walked to the park and sat on a bench under the trees. The next day he went to the station at the same time, in case he had muddled the day, but after an hour of strolling around he went home.

The following week he was back at São Bento to catch the early train to the Hospice. He had intended to try and tell Alfonso about Josefina, but now he knew there was little point. He sat with him in the communal garden as usual and tried to make him smile.

Raimund was stirring the cheese sauce. His cat, a grumpy ginger tom that had come with the apartment, jumped onto the worktop, tip-toed around the taps and put out a paw to catch the drips. It hissed at the sudden ringing; Raimund looked across at the phone; then switched off the gas. Not many knew his house phone number; and though ridiculous, but even after all these years, he was wary of the unexpected.

'*Sim*?'

'Raimund?'

'Yes?' He didn't recognise the voice.

'Thank God. It's Claire.'

'Claire?'

'Josefina's friend.'

'Josefina?'

'Yes. Look give me your address. I must come and see you.'

Again, rushing to cross a road, Josefina had not realised that the tram was beginning to move. She had tried to step back onto the pavement, but her knee gave way and the minibus had no time to stop. The first three months had been terrible. Her children had been at the hospital day and night, then just when everyone thought the worse, she had opened her eyes and said: 'Raimund.'

'Yes, she said "Raimund". Gee, can you believe it?'

Claire put down her cup and Raimund poured her another coffee. The cat jumped onto her lap and began purring. Raimund felt baffled. All this news about Josefina and then the cat being amiable.

'So that's when I started my detective work. God man, you were difficult to find.'

'Sorry.'

'Went back to your old university.'

'Surely not.'

'Yes, but that can all wait until later. I'm here to take you to Josefina.'

At first Raimund thought that the day room was empty, then he saw her sitting by the

French window. She held out her arms; he kissed her cheeks, her eyes, her ears; she clung to him.

'Need a hanky?' he asked.

'No, got one somewhere. Sorry about the sniffing.'

He pulled a stool next to her wheel chair and sat down.

'Sniff as much as you like my love.'

The dull winter was coming to an end. There were even days when it didn't rain; some mornings when Raimund stood on the balcony, Porto really looked as though it was ready for spring. His days were busy: visiting Josefina and Alfonso and then his trips up the coast to Praia Santo Antonio. Raimund was making plans.

'A few days by the seaside; that's what we both need,' said Raimund, and Josefina replied that he was mad. What did he want with a cripple?

He had said: 'I'm not wanting a cripple, I'm wanting you.' But he did not tell her all his plans.

Josefina's wheelchair was in the boot. The cat, that Josefina said must have a name and decided on *Laranga,* was in his basket.

The pink stripes in the sky were turning purple when they reached the villa. The cat had explored the garden and was now on the verandah washing his ears.

'I promised you we'd be here to watch the sun set and we made it.'

'You did, my love.' said Josefina and blew Raimund a kiss.

'*Laranga*,' She called to the cat.

He came and sat near her; she stroked his head; he looked up at her and then closed his eyes. Raimund poured out the wine, and laughed.

'*Laranga*! Orange! What a name for a cat.'

They touched glasses.

'To us,' said Raimund.

'To us.'

'Another surprise?' said Josefina. They were driving away from the coast, taking the one road up to the Serra d'Avis. The village café had been closed for the winter, but they saw the owner repairing an upstair's shutter. At the corner by the villagers' post boxes, Raimund stopped for a moment. He got out of the car and pushed in the side mirrors.

'Yes, this way, under the wisteria and we're there.'

The narrow track was fenced with tall trellis and they drove through a tunnel of amethyst blossom; petals dropped onto the bonnet of the car. The track ended on a grassy area; between a few boulders a rivulet of water was trickling. Then Josefina saw it. A one-storey granite house surrounded by oleander shrubs. At the front, a sloping path led up to an oak door; the three windows had white curtains looped across the panes. On one side of the house, and catching the morning sun was a balcony, and in the distance a deckled edge of mountains.

'Raimund. What a beautiful, beautiful spot. It's taken my breath away.'

'Do you want it?'

'Want it? What are you teasing me about?'

'It's yours. It's mine. It's ours.'

Josefina said. 'Where's my hanky? I'm always needing my hanky these days.'

Raimund wheeled Josefina across the garden and up to the front door. He handed her the key. Josefina unlocked the door.

'Wait,' said Raimund,'You know we can only live here under one condition.'

Josefina looked up at him.

'All those years ago you were going to be an artist ….'

'Oh, Raimund ...'

'I want you to be an artist here.'

Josefina reached up her arms and Raimund bent and kissed her neck.

'The first picture I will paint will be of …. '

'Me?'

'No. *Laranga*!'

Raimund kissed Josefina again.

*

Dear Reader

If you have enjoyed reading this book, then please leave a review on Amazon.
Thank you.

About The Author

Pam Finch has always enjoyed writing short stories, poetry and articles for publication, but this is her first book.
She also enjoys being creative with her sewing machine, but sometimes leaves home to tramp around Suffolk's lovely countryside.

Find out more about Pam please go to her blog
https://pamfinchwriter.wordpress.com/